BREWSTER

OHIO VAMPIRES BOOK 1

KATHI S. BARTON

This is a work of fiction. Names, characters, places, and incidents are products of the author's imagination or are used fictitiously and are not to be construed as real. Any resemblance to actual events, locations, organizations, or persons, living or dead, is entirely coincidental.

World Castle Publishing, LLC
Pensacola, Florida
Copyright © 2025 Kathi S. Barton
Hardback ISBN: 9798316568888
Paperback ISBN: 9798891263697
eBook ISBN: 9798891263703
First Edition World Castle Publishing, LLC, April 7, 2025
http://www.worldcastlepublishing.com
Licensing Notes
Cover: Cover Designs by Karen
Editor: Karen Fuller

Chapter 1

Brewster, Brew to his few friends, watched the party goers as they reveled down the streets. He didn't care all that much about their noise, but he didn't mind that they were out and about. Needing to feed, he decided that one or more of them — taking only a few sips of them — would fill his needs and would be perfect for him. Moving alongside the group, bringing the shadows around him, he tripped one of the partiers to have them slow just enough that he could get what he needed from them.

After getting his fill, putting money into their pockets, and leaving them none the wiser, Brew kept an eye on them so that nothing would befall them. With the slight loss of blood and their inebriated state, he would feel guilty if one of them were to fall and harm themselves. Once they were home, he left them to their night and made his way to his home. It wasn't that far, not with the ancient way that he could travel, but it was just as the sun was coming up, and he'd not meant to stay out that late.

Not that the sun would bother him. Being as old as he was and so full of magic, he could stand several days out in the sun without a single problem. However, it would drain him somewhat, and he didn't want to be caught unawares ever again. It was, he knew, dangerous for his kind to show too much in the way of magic without someone wanting a piece of it.

"Your lordship?" He told Landon that it was him. Then he asked him why he'd waited up. "It is my duty to make sure that you are well when you arrive home, and I take my duties seriously. What is it that you've been doing this night? Or do I want to know?"

"Would it matter that I don't want you to know?" Landon tsked at him. "I was out chasing rainbows and watching the stars dance on people's heads until it crushed them beneath its weight. Did you know that a comet will be coming by this way soon? Not too often does Ohio get anything special coming it's way." Again he tsked at him.

"I would think that you'd be better off in your office figuring out the next few businesses that you have under your rule." Brew told his man that he seldom ruled anyone. "If you say so. But we have been getting calls from that man again. The one that wishes for you to invest in his ideas so that he can expand."

"He'll just have to keep calling. I've told him a dozen times that I have no wish to invest in his schemes. They're farfetched and without any merit." Landon asked him what they were. "He believes that everyone should have free internet and phone service. While that is a good thing to wish, he wants me to foot the bill for it so that it's not a burden on others. I ask you, my man, what of my burden of paying for it? I have great riches but I do have an end to my money. I cannot afford to have everything that he wishes to put me out of — he also wishes for me to abolish all porn of adults and children. That has merit, but it is something that I don't think even the richest of all people could stop. It's there, and there is little to nothing a single person can do to make it disappear. It would take killing off anyone that has an ill thought. I fear that would kill about half the population, and then where would we be?"

"I see." He doubted that Landon understood anything that he'd said to him. The man had led a sheltered life the last thousand years as his man servant/butler. He didn't watch the television, never read a newspaper, nor had he been into town with him — ever — so that he'd get a firsthand look and feelings from the people out and about. If he were to take him to town, to the grocery store, the man would be terrified out of his mind with the things that people were doing. Poor man, he wouldn't survive a moment without someone there to bring him home, even after a few seconds.

Mayhap he wasn't correct in his assessment of his friend, but he liked the old man and would hate for anything to happen to him. And he also feared that there would be people out there who would take advantage of him, and that wouldn't bode well for him or his household. He liked the way things were and hated change in any way.

After sitting at his desk for an hour, he decided to go to his lair. Brew didn't know why he continued to call it that. It was a lovely bedroom with nice furniture in it. He even had his own bathroom so that he could shower and change while at home. Lying on his bed, he thought about the letter that he had received recently. It had to do with an old friend of his, Sirous.

They'd never had a use for a last name until recently. When pressed for one, Brew would simply say his name was Smith. He thought that anyone named Smith wasn't human. It was why the name was so popular. So many non-humans used it when they needed a last name. He knew, too, that Sirous was no different.

But Sirous was tired of this world and wanted to move beyond to the next. He hated to see that. He'd been there just recently, wanting to brush off the coils of this world himself. The two of them were bored and had no one around them to keep them busy. Also, he thought himself too old to change if someone did come along to shake up his world.

Just as the sun was at its peak, he closed his eyes. It didn't bother him, not at all, but he did need to rest and that seemed to be the best time to do so. Brew also knew that when he woke, the sun would still be in the sky, and he'd be in a better mood all the rest of the day.

Having the same dream…nightmare he supposed that would haunt him for days afterwards. The child that had snuck into his home was there. The woman with the most beautiful golden hair too. It had taken him a decade or more to realize that they were one and the same person. The child that had come into his home had grown up to be a beautiful creature that all mankind would seek. But he never saw their faces. Waking up, only his eyes widening, giving any indication that he had been stirred, Brew lay there, allowing his heart to slow and his fear to dissipate as well.

As he showered, he thought of the

nightmare. Once the child was in his home, she would flourish into a woman over the years. However, his dreams made it seem so quick. Like the time that she had entered and her adulthood was a single step into his house. Shivering, he thought of the rest of the dream while he stood under the warm spray.

"You shant come to me again, Beverly. I do not wish you in my bed." The child-woman laughed at him. The sound of it grating on his ears as he backed away from her. *"Do you not hear me? I said I will not have you in my chambers nor my bed. You are not anything to me."*

"What should it matter, Brewster? Who cares if we are not mated? No one. That's who. You shall take me to your bed and make love to me, then fill yourself. It is what I command of you as your –" and that was when he woke up.

He didn't know why it would make him wake in a cold sweat. Why her voice, above all others, made his skin crawl. The faceless woman would make him scream himself awake at times, bringing the household to his aid with guns and swords. There was so much about her that would, in a heartbeat, make him feel like he should run and hide rather than face her wrath.

Making his way to his office, he sat there at his desk with his computer, downloading the emails from today. It was like him to get a good start on things, but of late, all he wanted to do was roam the streets looking out for the faceless woman. Whatever she did or went, he needed to have an advanced look for her so as not to be caught unawares.

After paying the household bills, there weren't all that many of them, and even those weren't all that much, he looked at his investments. The electric bill was barely worth having it sent to him. They used no electric but for the kitchen and his room. None of his staff ate anymore because, long ago, it had gotten boring for them. The house had long since been paid off. The taxes were paid through the bank, so as he didn't have to bother with it. Then there were the cars that sat idle in the garage with no one to drive them, but they were kept up so that in an emergency, they would be there for anyone who needed them. His house ran itself, for which he was grateful. Not bothering him was the way that he liked it. As he sat there, reading emails, his mind wandered a little bit, and he was sorry that he was thinking of the dream again. What the hell did it mean? Who was she? And what hold did she have over him that made him so terrified?

Brew decided that he wasn't going to waste any more time on the dream. Whoever she was, if she even existed, he wasn't going to dream about her, nor was he going to speculate what she meant to him. He was finished. Done with her and her—the phone ringing startled him. He couldn't remember the last time it rang. Picking up the handset, he held it to his ear and waited.

"There are people out to get me, Uncle Daniel. Can you please just stop having me chased? It's my money left to me." He nearly told her that she had the wrong number when she started talking again. "I don't understand why you can take what was left to me. You've more money than sense anyway. Just fucking leave me alone."

The line went dead, and he wondered if the girl/woman he supposed was going to be all right. Looking at the phone, he put his hand back on the large handset and closed his eyes. It had been a very long time since he'd used this magic.

Reaching out beyond where he was, he found the apartment. It was a modest house with one bedroom and a living room that went into the kitchen. Four rooms, not counting the bathroom. As he began to search the house, he found the woman curled up on the floor between the living room and dining room table. She was crying. He could almost taste her tears, she was so upset. Willing himself to the room, careful that she didn't see him, he was first hit with the smell of the room, then the look on the woman's face when she looked directly at him.

"Who are you?" He didn't move, sure that there had to be a reason why she could see him. "You're not human, are you? Something... vampire. You're a vampire."

It was then that he noticed her face. It was marred by bruises. Blood was on her lips and her neck. Reaching out to touch her, she backed up further into the corner and stared at him. He told her that he meant her no harm.

"Yeah? Well, I've heard that before. As you can tell, I'm not all that trusting of that bullshit. How did you get in here?" He told her. "I guess I should have guessed that you'd have magic. Are you into shit with my uncle? He's out to get my money, though it's not nearly as much as he has."

Touching his finger to the large bruise on her face, he closed his eyes. As he reached out beyond them for the man, he was surprised that he'd gotten a good connection. Opening his eyes, keeping the connection to her uncle, he smiled. Not even bothering to hide his fangs.

"He is broke. More than that, he's had his home repossessed as well as his car. His bank account is overdrawn by several thousand dollars, and he hasn't anything to fall back on." She asked him what had happened. "He's been sued by his family. Your family as well, I suppose. Not only has he lost everything, but once the police find him, he'll be going to jail. For a good long time."

"What does this have to do with me?" He told her that he needed her money to buy his way out of jail by bribery. "I've been in this town for a while now, and I don't think the police would take all that kindly to him trying to bribe them. What makes you so sure about this? You have some kind of connection to my uncle?"

"Only through you." He reached out and put his hand on her shoulder. The connection was tight and strong. "You have a broken wrist and several broken ribs. The ones that aren't broken are bruised badly by what he has done to you."

"He found me just this morning. While I was trying to get me a bit of food to eat. He even took that from me, and until my next check comes, I don't have the money to...I do have money, but I won't touch it. It's my nest egg for a rainy day."

"You look as if a rainy day would blow

you over. Here, come to me. I will take you to the local hospital. While there, I'll make sure that no one knows that you're there. Just long enough for them to treat you." She told him that she had better things to do than to wait for hours in the emergency department, only to be told that she had no insurance and had to pay upfront. "They will not say such things to you whilst I'm there. I shall protect you."

Brew didn't know how he got her to the hospital. She was strong, but thankfully, he was stronger than her. She was battered, too. Her body was bruised from head to toe, like she was some kind of blue and gray person. Once she was in the little bed in one of the rooms, he turned off all the cameras that would show the two of them there, and as he had said, no one would be the wiser.

~*~

Calla watched the nurses as they fussed over her. It was nice, she thought, to have someone care so much about her. She knew too that it was only his magic, but for now, she was going to think it was because they were compassionate and good at their job.

"I didn't do anything to the nurses only to have them come to your aid. They're nice because you are." She told him to stop reading her mind. "Then you must speak to me when you have thoughts such as that. There are nice people in the world, but not many, I think, at times, but they are out there." He huffed at her. "You will stay here until you are better. I command it."

"Well, I don't take orders from a dick or a dictator. I'll leave when I wish." He growled low in his throat. "You don't scare me much. I don't know why, but you simply make me laugh when you get all huffy at me. What do you call your other self? I've known wolves that call their other self their better half. Or their beast, depending on what sort of shifter they are."

"You should be terrified of me. Also, you should listen to what I say to you. You've not done a very good job of keeping yourself well. You need a keeper to keep you out of harm's way." She asked him if he thought he was the person for the job. "I do believe that I am. You've no idea what sort of monsters are out there to prey on young women such as yourself."

"You think so? I have news for you... what is your name anyway? You come to my home, bully me into coming here, and I don't even know your name. Nor do you know mine either. It's Calla Lily Marshall. My grandmother declared me ugly at birth and thought a pretty name of a flower might make people not want to run from me when they saw me." He told her that was a lie. "I don't lie. I might want to tell a falsehood to someone, but I try very hard to be truthful. It's easier than trying to remember what you might have said to someone that wasn't true."

"No, I meant that your grandmother told you a lie. You are very beautiful. And you will look even more so when you have a bit of food in your belly more often." She laid back on the bed, wondering again why he was hanging around with her. She asked him. "I don't know why either. You're an irritant most of the little bit of time that I've been around you. You're too outspoken for your own good. And you're much too thin, as I pointed out to you before. Why does your uncle think that beating you will make you endeared to him?"

"I don't know that that's his plan. He told me once that he wished I was dead, but he can't seem to get me to die. I don't know why I haven't a few times. I've spent a lot of time in the hospitals because of him." Calla thought of the things that he'd told her when he was bashing her body into the pavement. "He thinks that I should be dead so that he can have all the money that I have without having to go through messing with me. I don't know why he thinks that I'll leave it to him. I've made out my will, and he's not mentioned other than to say that I'm not going to leave him anything. I'll donate the entire amount to the Red Cross instead."

"Notable charity." He asked her then how much she had. Without thinking that he could steal it all from her by his mo-jo, Calla told him. "That's a nice sum of money. As you might well know about my kind, I have a great deal of money, much more than I think that I even know about."

"That's just stupid. You should know all the time how much money you have." The nurse came in to give her something for the pain. They were going to stitch her up. "Don't leave me here alone. Please? I don't know why I trust you, but please don't leave me alone with my uncle still out there someplace."

"I shant leave you." He sat down in the chair just as the meds were kicking in. "Let it help you, Calla Lily. You'll feel better when you arise."

"What about your rising? Don't you need to rest?" She knew that her words were slurred, but she didn't want him to be a pile of dust when she woke up. "Go home. I forgot about you being what you are."

"I'm old. I'll be fine." If he said anything else, she didn't hear it. Just as she was starting to shut down her body, so relaxed, he spoke again. "My name is Brewster. Most call me Brew if they have known me for very long."

When she woke, he was just coming out of the bathroom. She knew next to nothing about his kind, but she didn't think that they went to the bathroom. Why that thought was there, she didn't have a clue. Of course, he'd have to use the bathroom. He was a —

"You're thinking too hard for someone who has slept for nearly four hours." She asked him if he used the bathroom. "Of course. Why would that even be a question? I'm still a person with a functioning body, am I not?"

"How the hell would I know?" She sat up better in the bed with his help. "I have to admit I do feel a good deal better. Tried still, but I'm sure that's just the meds they gave me."

"I helped you along in your sleep. I only put you into a deeper sleep so that you could rest. You stayed asleep for this long because I believe your body was just tired and needed it. Next time, please rest so that I don't have to intervene." She glared at him.

"I didn't ask you to intervene this time. You did that all on your own." She started to get out of bed, and he was suddenly there for her. The feeling of falling forward hit her hard, and it was all she could do not to be sick on him, too. "It would serve you right if I were to puke all over your nice suit."

She didn't think she'd been funny, but apparently, he thought so. His mirth was contagious, and she found herself smiling at him. That was when she noticed that his eyes were so beautiful. Almost a clear blue. Like the sky in the summer. Blue as the moon that was full through the fall. Christ, she thought, a person could fall for him with just that. He asked her what she was thinking.

"The color of your eyes." He moved back from her when she was settled. "I want to see your beast or whatever it is you call him. Don't ask me why. I have no idea why I want to see him, but I want…no, I don't know why either, but I need to see him."

He stepped back from her, and she thought that he was going to tell her no. Instead, he took off his jacket and shook his body. Before she could beg him this time, his body stretched out, elongated to the point where he was taller than he had been. She'd bet he was at least eight or nine feet tall. His face was usually full and clean-shaven, but for the mustache that he wore elongated as well, stretching until he was almost gaunt-looking. His ears became pointed, sharp-looking against his head. But it was his eyes that mesmerized her. They were dark now, blood filled with only a hint of the ones that she felt so good about before.

Lifting his hands, she could see that his fingers were longer. The nails at the end were about four or five inches long and deep red. There was nothing beautiful about him. Oddly enough, she thought him to be handsome yet deadly. When he took a step toward her, then another, she didn't flinch away but put out her hand to touch him.

The monster, the only thing that she could think of, rubbed his face along her hand and then up her arm to her shoulder. When he nuzzled at her neck, Calla let him do so, even tilting her head so that he could do with her as he wanted. Licking along her throat, she knew on some level he was going to bite her, and it was going to hurt. Calla came hard when he sank his teeth, his long, sharp teeth, into her tender neck.

She must have passed out at some point because when she opened her eyes, he was sitting in the chair he'd been in before, staring at her. Feeling self-conscious, she asked him if he was all right. Nodding once, he told her that he'd never been better and asked after herself.

"Fine. A little lightheaded but just fine. What happened?" He just stared at her like he was seeing her for the first time. "Are you all right?"

"I'm several thousand years old." She nodded. "In all that time, I never once had anything to do with humans, as I thought them to be greedy and selfish. Then, just as I was thinking of joining the others of my kind who have become bored with life, someone comes along and rattles my bones."

"You're not making any sense." He stood up, and she nearly backed away from him when he came toward her. But holding herself still, he licked along her cheekbone to get a drop of her blood, he told her. "What's going on? Why are you being particularly odd right now?"

"You did this to me. You've settled in my heart so that I cannot now nor ever turn to ash. I'm not mad, but I am feeling a little off." She nodded, still not sure as to what he was talking about. "You're my mate, Calla Lily. One that I never thought I would find in all my days as I grew older. You have given me something that I've never had before. A look on life—"

"Hold on there a second. Just give me a minute." He nodded, his smile not very comforting to her at the moment. "I can't be your mate. I'm just a human. And you've made it clear to me that you don't care for us. Humans, I mean."

"I've changed." She said she wasn't sure that had anything to do with her. "It has everything to do with you. And you are no longer just a human. You've become so much more in the moments that I drank from you."

"Take it back." Brew said that he could not. "You did something to me. Whatever it is, I…You did this, and you can take it back."

"I cannot. I don't even know now that I want to. You are my mate for all times. And by the way, you weren't wholly human before I claimed you. You have a bit of vampire in you from somewhere back in your lineage. A little wolf as well." Shaking her head, he only nodded. "You've healed as well. And you'll stay healthy for the rest of our days together. Did you know that you had spots of cancer throughout your body? You would not have lasted more than a year had I not claimed you."

"You said that twice now. What do you mean you've claimed me?" He explained it to her. "No, I didn't…well, I did, but I think that I was just horny and needed some relief. Why are you laughing? This isn't funny."

"No, 'tis not. But I find myself wondering if you will be like this our entire life." She told him that there wasn't going to be an entire life with him. "So you say. But I have a feeling that once you are in my home — our home you will feel differently. I know that I'm looking at it as a home now and not a place to rest. A house with no warmth but for you."

"You're getting ahead of yourself there, bucko. I didn't say I was going anywhere with you." He laughed again, a short, sharp laughter that made her think that he was just as surprised by it as she was. When he stood up, putting his hands out, she didn't know whether to take it or not. "You're not going to let me be alone, are you?" He shook his head, his face still covered in humor. "I don't want to be your mate, Brew. It's not going to be good for either of us. It's going to be bad."

"Not so long as I have breath in my body. And before you ask, yes, I have breath in me. But you and I, we'll do well together. Have a good life. I'll take care that your uncle no longer bothers you again." She asked him if he was going to kill him. "If it comes to that, I will, but for now, I'm going to try and talk to him about his hurting you. May I hurt him? As he has you? That would satisfy both myself and my monster. For now."

She didn't want to ask him what that meant. Being all right with him hurting him seemed to make her think that since he wasn't anything but human, he might not survive a beating. Instead, she nodded and took his hand.

When she opened her eyes, not sure when she'd closed them, she was no longer in the hospital but now in a home. Even from the front entrance, she knew it to be a large mansion. One that she'd never be able to walk around in a single day.

"This is our home. Our staff is just beyond in the kitchen. I believe they will enjoy having you around." She asked him if they would bite her as well. "No. They're ancients, as I am, but they no longer have the need to eat. I think that will change with you among them. I believe, at least, I hope you will keep them on their toes much like you will me."

"I'm still not sure about this. You'll keep your teeth behind your lips, or I'll stake you in the middle…when you go to bed. I'm assuming you have to sleep?" She thought of something then, something that she'd read. "Can you only drink from me? I've read that someplace."

"Nay, I can feed from anyone should I wish. I don't want to because you come so prettily when I feed from you. I'd like to do that again, though I have no need to. To hear you screaming out your climax, calling my name when you do. It makes me hard just to think about it."

"No more of that." He looked like a small child that had missed his nap. Brew's lower lip hung out there, and she felt the need to bite him, take that wet lip, and nibble on it until she needed to come again. Turning her back to him, she headed to what she had hoped was the kitchen. The man was in for a rude awakening if he tried that shit on her again. But her body tingled when she thought of how delicious she had felt coming the way that she had.

Chapter 2

Daniel didn't care for having to look for his niece. She should just stay where she lived, and that would be the end of it. Why she worked was beyond him, but he was also glad for it because it gave him extra cash when he was low on it. Also, he loved knocking her around. She was strong and seemed to bounce back quickly, and it gave him a thrill to watch the blood seep out of her body, and the marks showing up made him feel like a big man, beating the underlings of the world.

He was sitting outside her apartment complex when one of the cops sounded their sirens at him to get him to come to their car. Daniel hated all kinds of authority, but the police were his least favorite. If they got a burr up their asses about something, they could make your life a living hell. That's one of the reasons that he was polite to them as well as avoided them every time he went out.

It surprised him to no end that he wasn't taken in for questioning about Calla all the time. She must not be talking to the cops when he knocked the fuck out of her. Either that, or they didn't care for her either, and that was what he was counting on. It was simply too much fun for him to have at her expense to get a little cash than to let her go on living. The fucking cunt.

Daniel didn't work unless it was wholly required of him. Which meant that he didn't have anyone to be beholding to and did as little as possible when he was flush. He supposed that working his fists on Calla was working, but it was fun, so he didn't bitch about it too often. And never to her.

Not understanding why his mom had left everything to Calla, he did get bits and pieces of her money when he could. The stupid bank people didn't say anything when he brought her into the bank with him to get some of her cash. The thing was, they had a limit on how much she could take out a day, and he'd always forget to take her back daily so he could have the two grand each time. Of course, when he knocked her around, he knew that she had to be laid up someplace to get healed, but that was something he was going to make sure that he did daily when he found her again. Waiting around on the money in only pocket change was making things difficult for him. And it was always about him, damn it. Now this.

"Yes, sir, what can I do for you?" The office told him to hang on a moment, he had something for him. "Hopefully, it's from my niece, Calla Marshall. She's been neglecting paying back the loan that I lent her last year."

"I don't believe that she owes you anything, Mr. Marshall. This is from the man that she's going to marry. And he asked me to be sure that I explained to you fully that she's under his protection and that if he sees a single mark on her, he'll not ask questions but hunt you down. I'd take heed to that, sir. Mr. Smith is a man that no one messes with a second time." He asked if the man had just threatened him. "I'd not say that was a threat but more like a promise for you. He will hurt you if you don't leave her alone. Also, I'm to tell you too that her money is no longer your concern. He's made arrangements at the bank that no one but himself and her can get to it."

"So he's taking her to the cleaners? I pay my taxes and —" The officer said that he wasn't paying taxes actually and that he had a court hearing date for him to have that taken care of as well. "I don't own anything around here, so why would I have to pay taxes on it."

"The same reason that you don't own the cops. There will be no more blind eyes to her walking about beat to shit, either. When she tells us about you, we'll be running you in." He said what changed. "Mr. Smith is what's changed. He donates a great deal of money to our city, and he said that the donations would stop immediately if she's hurt again, and we allowed you to go around like you didn't do it. He's made it very clear that he's disappointed in us for allowing it to go on this long."

"Well, she's related to me through marriage. If he has a problem with me and her getting together, I'm going to have to have a talk with him." The officer — he couldn't see his name tag right then — told him he'd be smart and just do as he was told. "So you're afraid of one man, and that's going to curtail my fun. I don't think you're seeing the larger picture here. She owes me money, and I plan to get it."

"It's your funeral." He didn't like that and told the man that. "Whatever, Mr. Marshall. He's a very wealthy man who isn't going to be taking shit from you. As I said, if I were you, I'd just forget about it and get myself a job. Everybody is hiring, and that might save you from being dead."

"Is there anything else? If not, I'm going to be on my way." He was handed the envelope with his name on it, and he had to sign that he'd taken it. Whatever. He knew that shit like this would never stand up in court, so he wasn't worried about it. Sitting back on the bench, he wished daily that he still had his car where he could at least enjoy some air conditioning. This heat was for the birds.

Sitting down, he tried to think if he had

any cash on him, not wanting to move again for breaking out in a sweat. He did remember having about two hundred dollars on him but he'd gone out last night and had him a big meal. My god, it was wonderful to be waited on and have a steak dinner, too. That's when he realized that he had about a fiver on him and nothing more. The good kind of beers were eight bucks a bottle nowadays, and he didn't have that much. If he had to drink that nasty shit again, he was going to puke on himself. But he needed a drink, and that was going to have to do.

After getting back with his beer, glad when a twenty had been in his pocket so that he could have the better stuff, he did think about the fact that if he'd bought the cheap beer, he could have had four to just being able to have two but it was a no brainer, and to him, it was the principle of the thing.

There had been no one stirring at Calla's apartment now for three days. Usually, she was up and around, going to that job she had by now. If she didn't come out of there tomorrow, he was going to have to go up to her place and wrestle her out. He had things to do, and her sitting around on her lazy ass healing wasn't working for him. She owed him money.

Calla didn't really owe him shit. When his mother had died about six months ago now, everything had been left to his brother's kid. Charles had been dead for about ten years now, which meant that it went directly to her rather than probate like it did. He could contest things then, but with her directly getting the money and house and the will mentioning that he didn't get squat because of his dealings with a bad group of people, he couldn't lie his way around that either. He finally pulled out the letter to read. No one was going to make him read anything on their time if he could get by with it. Stupid shithole more than likely was going to spell his name wrong too.

"Mr. Marshall." The handwriting looked elegant. Not a word that he used all that much. But it looked like someone with a fancy hand had written. "More than likely from some old queer."

"Mr. Marshall, I'm writing you to warn you — giving you full notice — that if you bother my wife, Calla Lily Marshall Smith, at any time going forward, I will hunt you down. Calla Lily has given me permission to harm you should you hurt her again, and that will hold me from killing you. But if she is hurt and unconscious, I will assume that once again you wished to kill her, and I will make you suffer in ways that will make you wish for death.

"I'm a very wealthy man who has nothing to do but to pamper my Calla Lily, and by that, I mean that keeping her safe is a priority to me. If you harm a single hair on her head, cause her any undue pain, I will kill you. If she tells me that you have stressed her in any way, I will kill you. I'm sure that you see a pattern emerging here. Leave her alone, or I shall not hesitate in making you nothing but fertilizer for someone's yard."

Then it was signed Brewster Smith with Calla's signature under his. Wadding the paper up, he dug it out of the trash can to use it as proof when he had to kill the man himself. He had threatened him no less than four times, and he wasn't going to put up with that. Crossing the street, he made his way to Calla's place and went upstairs to her apartment. Pounding on the door, he would wait until she opened it, his fist curled up, and his anger just as hot as he could get it. He might think of himself doing a favor for the other man and kill her for him. He knew Calla and she wasn't that big of a prize for anyone. Momma had always said that she was ugly. By god, he was going to make her less attractive with his —

"What the hell are you pounding on that door for?" He told the neighbor that he was looking for his niece. "Nobody lives there no more. Movers came in and helped them Goodwill people load up all her stuff and take it away."

"She does, too, live here. Go back into your house and leave me be. Stupid cunt. I know where she lives." She told him that she was going to get her ball bat and she'd show him what a cunt could do. When she went into her house, closing the door behind her, he pounded on the door again. "Calla, get your fucking ass here and open the door. I'm about as pissed off as I've ever been before. And what makes you think you can sic someone on me when I'm just trying to get what you owe me."

"She don't live here." Another neighbor was yelling at him. "Damn it all to hell. If you wake my baby, you're going to get a nice ear ringing from me. You've been told twice now that she don't live here no more."

He heard the sirens then and was happy to be able to have someone else arrested. Just as he was turning to talk to the second neighbor, he was hit from behind with something hard. The second time it hit him in the back, he saw stars and hit the floor. Somebody was hurting him, and he didn't like it.

When he woke up, he was in the emergency department on one of those hard-as-ass beds that weren't nearly wide enough for a man his size. Not that he was fat, he told himself, but he wasn't narrow either. Mother fuck. Someone was going to—lifting his arm to call a nurse, he couldn't believe it when he figured out he was chained to the bed. This shit was getting old, and he was going to make sure someone paid for this. Instead of calling one of the nurses on the call button, he started yelling for someone to get their asses in there and undo him. His head was hurting. He was so pissed off.

"Shut up." He eyed the woman who had come into the room where he was. "You beller like that again, and I'm going to make sure that the hits that you had coming to you were nothing. Shut your ever-loving mouth."

"You can't talk to me like that. I want you to take these off of me right now." She said she wasn't a cop, and they were the ones that put it on him. "Well? Get off your ass and get me one. I don't like being chained like an animal."

"Yet you act like one. Mr. Strouse is the one who called us when you started yelling at a closed door. Didn't they tell you a bunch of times that she wasn't there? I know they did. Then you went and woke up his baby girl. They've got enough going on there without you adding to it. Ms. Tailor is the one that hit you, and if'n I'd been here, I would have bashed in your empty skull had I been there." She got close enough to him that he could count her nose hairs. That had him backing away from her. "You make one more peep before you're released, then I'm going to find me a big male nurse and have them do a rectal probe on you. Got it?"

"Yes, ma'am." He was terrified that she'd do just what she said, so he kept his tone down. "Where are the police that locked me down? If you don't mind me asking you to find them for me, I'd appreciate it, please?"

He'd never groveled in his life, yet here he was, a grown assed man working the women in front of him like she was going to pull out a gun and shoot him in the nuts. And that was what he felt like, too, that she had his nuts in one of those fancy nutcrackers he would see at Christmas time.

~*~

Brew watched the man in the small bed. He'd been here since he woke up and bitching about things and didn't think that he liked the man any better than he had before meeting him. He was repulsively fat, weighing in at he'd bet four hundred pounds. He dressed like a man who was half his weight, and that made him think that the man had no qualms about eating too much at every meal. He knew there was nothing wrong with the man that would have him being that heavy other than he just didn't care.

He'd gotten a taste of the man when he'd heard about the incident at the apartment complex. Leaving word that someone would call him if he returned had been a good investment. Now all he had to do was to wait for him to screw up again, and he'd be out of his love's hair. And he did love Calla Lily, too.

She'd been at his home for four days now. After making sure it was all right with her if he were to close out her other place, he donated all the things in the apartment to the Goodwill Store. Calla Lily had told him that there was nothing there but terrible memories, and she wanted to make new ones. He was fine with that and told her as much.

"Your house is very stiff, isn't it?" He told her that was the problem; it was just a place where he rested. "I've noticed that you have most of the house shut off. Is there a reason for that, too?"

"None. Other than the staff doesn't need to clean those rooms and I had them close them off to avoid them. It's worked out well for us." She told him that other than Landon, his butler and man's man, the other staff were useless. "They've been with me for so long that they are more than likely taking advantage of me. Yes, I'll agree. But as I said, they've been with me for so long they've become a part of the house."

"They're a part of something all right. Did you know that Mary comes in and clocks in, then leaves only to return at five to clock out? She does this daily, I'm told." He asked her what she did if not working for him. "As far as I've been able to see, she goes home and works there. Getting double the paycheck is putting a great deal of money in her pockets. The same goes for Olivia, who was trained by Mary and does the same thing. Only she doesn't bother coming in at all but gets paid like the others."

"I didn't know that." She nodded, he remembered, then pulled out a notebook and told him what all the staff was doing. The cook, she told him, was dead, and he'd been paying her family her wages for the last twenty-five years. "They've been collecting it because she was killed in some way that I would have been responsible?"

"No. She was robbing a church with her sister, who was also killed and was caught stealing. She only got about forty-five dollars and a bullet in her head when she thought it would be easy money like she'd been getting from you." He sat down, thinking that he should do what she said and pay attention to his money. "Four months ago, you gave her a raise."

"I'm guessing that Landon has told you all this." She told him that he'd not wanted to, but she'd asked him. Thinking that there should have been more people working here. "He's a good man. I'm assuming that he's tried to tell me this before."

"On several occasions." Calla Lily sat down at the table with him, but not close enough for him to touch her. "You should be more careful with your money, Brew. I know that I have no room to talk about money, but mine was being stolen from me by a man who beat me up. Yours is being stolen right under your nose."

"Are you planning to take me to the — never mind. That was a cruel question, and I don't believe you have any interest in my money other than for me to keep it in my vault and bank." She said that she was bored and needed something to occupy her mind. "I'm assuming that you went to Landon and asked him about the people working here. Thank you for that."

"They're all gone now. He said you told him that he was in charge of the house, and he fired them all. Stopped payments on the checks that were to go out for people that don't actually work for you." Again, he thanked her. "I have a couple of questions for you."

"Anything, love. Anything at all." She told him he didn't know what it was yet. "I would lay down my life for you. Not for what you've done for me already but the things I think you're going to be doing for us in the future."

"I want to have control of the household accounts." He said they were hers. "Thank you. Also, I'd like to do something other than just sit around your lovely home too. I'm bored, and when I'm bored, I tend to do things that I don't usually ask permission to do. Like, I've already started on the herb garden out back. Also, it looks as if someone at one time tried to grow a vegetable garden. While I don't want to spend all day snapping peas and green beans, I would like to have some for my own dinner. No one here knew how to cook either."

"With you here, I'd like to entertain again. This used to be the place to have large gatherings. While I don't care for the human race, I do enjoy the company of some of my kind. Not to live here, but to be here for occasions where I must dress up." She eyed his clothing, and he laughed. He'd been doing that, laughing again, for a while now, and he would swear that it took years off his body. "I mean in a man's tux with all the women in long flowing dresses. Dressing to the nines, I believe it was called at one time. Yes, I'd like to get the house opened up again and show you off to them."

"I'm not all that much to show off, Brew." She flushed brightly, and he had to smile. He might well have said nothing if he thought she was fishing for compliments, but she was stating a fact that she'd been told all her life. But to him, she was everything. "I also wanted to talk to you about us being together. I know you told my uncle that we were married, but we're not. Is there a way that we can make that true so that no one takes exception to it if they find out? No wedding is necessary, but if you could have it put to the record, I'd be happy with that."

"It has been filed. I did not tell you when it was done as you were still getting used to the things around here. Had I known how much of an investigator you were, I might well have

waited for you to figure it out on your own."
They both laughed, which was what he'd been
going for. He worried that it would upset her
as he'd done it without telling her. "There
are many things that I have done since, too.
I have put your name upon the deeds to the
houses and property that we now own. Credit
accounts. I have even made it so that your
money is in a safe place where your uncle will
no longer have access to it. I believe the bank
will now fully cooperate with you in keeping
his fingers out of your accounts."

"I hope so. Like I said, it's a lot of money
that I was saving for a house." She started to
turn away but looked at him. "Will you put
that money with yours now? I would like for
you to do that. You've given me so much that
I want to contribute as much as I can as well."

He didn't tell her that simply being
around was more than he'd ever hoped for,
and just being able to gaze at her at any time
he wished was a perk he'd not counted on. The
very fact that she was saving him a great deal
of money was, again, nothing that he'd ever

thought of.

"It would be my pleasure to invest your money with ours. And anytime you need anything, you've only to ask Landon or myself, and we'll get it for you." Her face flushed again, and he found it to be the most endearing thing he'd ever captured in a woman's face. Yes, he thought to himself. He was one lucky vampire. "We'll need to hire a full staff. Open the rooms up that have been closed off for no other reason than it was easier on someone else to do so." He thought about the rooms in the house. "I wouldn't be able to tell you what a single room has in it, much less the color of the paper. I do believe the last time they were opened up, it was when wall coverings were all the rage."

"It might be better to hire someone to come in and clean the rooms then. It's doubtful if they look as bad as I'm thinking, but we don't want our new staff running for the hills after opening one of the doors." He laughed with her again. "I know it sounds as if I'm just sliding into this with no thought to how long we've known one another, but I'm thinking about everything that I do. I'm not one to go willy-nilly into things, and it seems like that to me. But I'm not. I'm calculating every move I make to make sure that if you were to ever want to rid yourself of me, then I will be able to stand on my own two feet and survive. I'll be broken, but I won't die of starvation or lacking a place to live."

"I'm glad that you're prepared, love. But I shan't ever leave you. You are my heart and soul. My very life." She just stared up at him, her eyes filling with unshed tears. "Oh, my heart. I will make it my life's work to make sure that you understand that I love you so much."

The rest of the afternoon and up until dinner, Brew pampered Calla Lily. She was strong, there was no doubting that, but she was just like the flower that she was named for. A delicate flower that blooms with its whole stem. Something so fragile that it begged to be protected. Yet, like the flower, she was strong and resilient. And he loved her with all of his heart.

After dinner, she had made herself a

grilled cheese with some pasta on the side. He'd explained to her that she'd never gain weight unless she was breeding. He loved that she ate what she wanted, and he was happy with her sigh of relief that she could, if she wished, have children now. He supposed that being alone, she'd never given it a single thought. Now, she seemed to be thrilled to start on that chapter.

"Not today." He nodded. "You have to believe me when I tell you that I'm happy with you here. Also, I'm falling in love with you. But not yet. I have some nightmares of my own that haunt me, and he's still running around like he's nothing to worry about. Did I tell you that he went to the bank?"

"I heard, too. I guess it was quite a surprise for him not to be able to get to any of your money when he'd been told that very thing. The police were called." She said she thought that was the best part. "He was taken to jail and stayed overnight until they were able to get to the bottom of him not having any cash. It was quite the eye opener for the police, too, that it happened so quickly for him to try to access your money so soon after being told it wasn't his."

"Peter Lanne said that he'd had a fit that he wasn't being treated nicely as he had some money in my accounts. Can you imagine the look on his face when he was told to get out and to never return? I bet he doesn't give up, either. He told Peter that I'd given him the access all along and that it was unfair of me to take it from him this late in the game. Daniel has nearly five dollars on himself that is going to have to last him until he gets a job or some other form of payment that isn't me." Brew told her that he'd had twenty. He'd slipped it into his pocket when he took a sip of him to know where he was at all times. "I heard that he spent his last few bucks on some kind of drink. It figures, Daniel has always thought that he deserves the finer things in life. Even if he couldn't afford them. It is a small wonder that Grannie didn't leave him anything. He was forever 'borrowing' from her. She kept track of his borrowing, too, right up to the penny. When she passed away, he owed her over a hundred grand in cash, and then there were the things that he'd stolen from her that he pawned or sold off. Jerk. Grannie took great care of me when I was younger. I hated to see her go."

"I knew her when she was but a child, your grandmother. She was much like you, insecure yet strong. When her baby had been born, she had nothing to do with his upbringing because her husband wanted to raise him in the way that he was. That didn't turn out very well, and when he died, having a heart attack one night when he'd been yelling at Daniel about his waste of money, she turned her back on him. He stole things from her like he did you. I think she did well in not leaving him anything." Calla Lily said that she thought so, too. "Good. To change the subject, we'll have to have a trip soon. I need to be in New York for a meeting, and it would be my pleasure to have you with me. Would you like that?"

"I believe that I would." He was happy with her answer. He didn't know what he'd do if she didn't go with him. He'd been looking forward to showing her off for a few days now, and New York was the perfect place to do so.

Chapter 3

The dress, that's what she was calling it, the dress fit her like a glove. And even though she had plucked it off the rack herself, someone would think that it had been made especially for her slim body. The pretty sequins all over the dress made her sparkle and shine. Her shoes, black again, had the tiniest red bow on them, and the shawl that had come with the dress covered her from head to toe like she was some kind of creature of the dark. The dress made her feel like she'd never felt before. Pretty. Sexy.

"Are you ready, my love?" She told him that she just needed a moment and that she'd be out. "I do hope you're not getting cold feet again. I have it on good authority that the dress will fit you well and that people will be wondering where I got such a lovely wife. Which reminds me. I have something for you finally. I've been waiting for it to come back from the cleaners."

She stepped out of the room with her cape over her dress. He said that he had wanted to be surprised like the others at the ballroom would be. She would have thought that he'd want to see how she was dressed before they left so that she'd have time to change. Into what? She didn't have a clue as this was the only dress that she'd gotten today.

Taking her hand into his much larger one, she was startled when he kissed her hand and slipped what she could only assume was a ring onto her finger. Lifting it up in the bright light, it sparkled around the room much like her dress had.

"It's beautiful, Brew." And it was. The diamond in the middle of the ring was a brilliant white. The prisms that danced from it made up all the colors of the rainbow. The row of blue and red gems surrounding it just made the large diamond sparkle more. It was as if she'd been given the buttons to push on fireworks, and they were lighting the evening splendor of the room. All she needed to hear was the booms, and she'd swear that she was at a Fourth of July party and she'd been right under the lights.

"Come on now before I convince you that we need not go and the two of us get to know one another in a more personal way." Before she could figure out what he was saying, she was in a large black limo, and it was speeding down the road from the hotel they were in. "How have you liked New York so far? I remember when it was nothing more than shanty houses along the banks and lovely flowers blooming all around it. Such an odd time of my life. I never cared for the larger cities. Too many people around. But Ohio? Well, it's been my home for the last few centuries, and I can't imagine living anywhere else. Especially with you by my side."

"I've been to New York City before. I was only a kid. I remember thinking that people were faster here. They seemed to have more purpose in their steps but had nowhere to be. I was just a kid then, but it all seemed to be something out of a science fiction book that I used to read." She laughed and told him that she'd been a very strange kid. "I love to read. That's why I can't wait to get back home and read every book in your library. Landon told me that you also like to read and that you have a lot of first editions in your home. What was it like meeting all those famous authors before they were…well, famous?"

"Some were already famous, as you might have guessed, but there were a few that I enjoyed an easy conversation with when they were in a pub or somewhere that I happened to be. Ah, here we are now."

The building was magnificent and brightly lit up. As she was handed out of the limo, her leg slid out onto the pavement like she'd practiced all afternoon. Standing up, she looked into Brew's eyes when he didn't move and saw something there that she'd never seen on a man's face when he was looking at her. Lust. Need and something that she couldn't put her finger on. Love perhaps? She didn't know but continued to stare at the man she just then realized that she loved.

"Brew?" They were whisked into the building, and he held onto her like she was his lifeline. Or he was hers. Calla didn't know, but she knew too in those few moments before entering the massive building that she could never tell Brew in words how much she dearly loved him. When he suddenly stopped moving, reaching for her cape, she leaned up to his face and kissed him on the cheek. "I love you so much."

"Christ, your timing couldn't be worse. But this will be fun, I think. I shall make you suffer for this. In a wonderfully sexual way." He turned her around and took off the cape. When his lips touched her ear, she leaned into him and laid her head on his chest. "I could find us a dark corner or make us one if you keep this up. My goodness, this is going to be a hard, very hard night." He rolled his hips, and she could feel his cock as it touched off every cell in her body. His laughter had her giggling. His curt *"behave"* had her laughing harder. Then he turned her around and looked at her.

Her dress fit her differently than it had in their hotel room. It was as if her body had shifted around. Her breasts were larger, and her nipples seemed to have taken a mind of their own. The slit up the side seemed to be exposing every part of her. Her back, bare to his touch now, felt like he was pressing her against something hard and hot. She knew that it was only his hand but it too felt different touching her. Her body, it seemed, was on fire for this man, and she didn't care who knew it.

"Mr. Cunningham, thank you for inviting us to your lovely party. I don't think you've met my wife, Calla Lily Smith." He kissed her hand, and she heard Brew growl deep in his throat. She had to shift around, her pussy feeling soaked right now from the man talking. "We've only been here for the last few hours, and people have been so welcoming."

"And they should. You're a good man, Brewster. A good man to have around, too." He looked at her, then away, like he'd been caught with his hand in the cookie jar. "Very lovely. You have a very lovely wife, too."

He hurried away, and she looked at Brew. "You scared him. Or something. What did you do to that poor man?" He told her. "You're going to have every male in his place running from me by showing them what you're going to do to them if they look too hard at me. You need to behave."

"Had I even looked at this dress at the hotel, we wouldn't have left the bedroom for a decade. I plan on making you pay for your beauty tonight by teasing you every minute that I can. I shan't let you out of my sight either. you need a keeper, young lady." She told him that every woman in the place was younger than him, and he kissed her quickly on the mouth.

Calla had to acknowledge that she was having fun as well. He would whisper how he'd met the people coming to them, and she would be hard-pressed to keep a straight face. Some of his stories were outrageous enough that he had to be making them up. Others she just found humorous. Like their hostess.

"Ms. Taylor, before becoming Mrs.

Cunningham, was quite the flirt. Also, the dancer. I remember once going to a club that featured women dancers, and there she was up on the stage doing the can-can. She could lift that leg of hers up to a man's chin. I remember that very well, too." She just stared at him. "You don't think me to be a virgin after living as long as I have, did you?"

"No, I guess not, but you don't have to brag about it." He told her that he was sincerely sorry. "It's all right. I just…I'm insecure enough, I think."

"You've no reason to be. The women in this room cannot hold a candle to your beauty. All the men and some of the women are jealous of me having you by my side." She looked around again. Before, she thought they were staring at him, but now she could see that Brew was right. They were staring at her. "You're so fresh to all of this that I fear they'll try to get you to join some clubs or some such nonsense and tear you away from me."

"Never." He turned her to him and stared at her. Calla let him look all he wanted to. She wanted him to know that she not only loved him but trusted him as well. "I love you, Brew."

"And I do you, my heart." The rest of the evening was spent going from one couple to the next. He knew everyone at the party and told her bits and pieces about their lives and what they did for a living. It was so much information, but she had no trouble remembering it all. Brew even knew bits and pieces about the staff as well.

On their way back to the hotel, she slipped her heels off. Her feet were a little sore, but with one touch from Brew, they felt like she'd been barefooted all evening. Curling up next to him on the drive, she fell asleep in seconds. His scent seemed to lure her into a deep sleep.

Waking up the next morning, she was alone in the big bed — and not just any bed but the one at their home. It looked as if she'd been alone in the bed all night and got up disappointed. After getting out of bed and into the shower, she was glad that she'd slept alone. Her body was sore from the tips of her toes to the top of her hair. As soon as she was able to get out of the hot spray and wash the pens out of her hair, she did feel marginally better.

"Good morning, miss. My name is Hattie. I'm the new cook." She said she was glad to meet her. "Your husband said to tell you that he'd be back this afternoon and that something had come up, and he couldn't get out of it." She laughed like it was the funniest thing in the world to have him gone. Then she explained. "I understand now why he told me to have you eat a hardy breakfast and lunch. The wind could carry you away, I think."

"I'm a bit on the tiny side." She was handed a cup of tea and pushed it aside. Tea, especially hot, wasn't anything that she went out of her way for. She could drink it, but she didn't care for it all that much."

"How about cold tea? Do you like it? Sweet or unsweet?" Again, she told her that she could drink it but preferred very cold water with ice. "That's easy enough to fix. I take it you don't drink coffee either, then?"

"No, I don't. I couldn't afford it before,

so I never acquired a taste for it. I much prefer to have juice in the morning with water for the rest of the meals. Wine, too, but since I don't drink it often, it tends to make me a little loopy when I do." They talked for around an hour about the things that she liked and disliked. There wasn't too much on the latter list, but she didn't care all that much for heavy meals. Unless, of course, it was for comfort, and that's all she wanted. Calla told her that any meal that was called comfort food had at least eight items on it, and they were all deep-fried. The two of them laughed at that for the next twenty minutes.

"I love mashed potatoes. They don't even have to have gravy on them for me to eat them. I like chicken fried steaks with the mentioned potatoes, green beans, peas, corn, and zucchini. Then, there has to be either cornbread or home-baked bread. Apple or cherry pie and plenty of ice-cold water." Hattie told her that she sure did love fresh butter beans, too, and Calla agreed. "Those have to have a ton of melted butter on them so that they're overcooked in it.

I've not had those in years."

"I'll tell you what, I'll make you some up for dinner tonight." She said that she'd eat that all by herself. "Good. Then I'll make sure to have plenty on hand."

When Brew returned home, she could tell that something had happened. As they were seated in his office, he finally told her about his friends who were coming to visit them. He seemed so sad in that moment.

"Sirous is the one that I'm worried about most. We were together in a lot of wars and things that go on with humans. Yosef is another friend of mine that both Rance and Rutger recruited to hang out with us. You'd never know to meet them, but they're the most shy men that I've ever met. Moreso than even you are." She asked him where they were. "The only one I know for sure is Sirous. He had been visiting his father's estate the last few months. There were some problems with his will, but he's gotten it all straightened out now. Kenneth lives overseas. I think he's more British than American now. I think he runs an art gallery. Most of the work is his, but he doesn't tell anyone that. I don't know that he tries very hard to sell any of his things either."

"Do you have any family left?" He said just his friends. His father was killed one night when it was found out they were vampires, and his mother never came around anymore. "I bet that was a scary time for you all. I know that books make you guys seem like you're all nice people, but I'm betting that's not true either."

"It's not. There are more of us that are bad, as you called them, than nice ones, but they know better than to try anything with the older vamps." She asked him about baby vampires. "They have an entirely different set of rules that they must follow. As you can imagine, most of them don't, and they have to be put down. A great many of them don't make it the first couple of months, thinking that being a vampire is sexy and full of riches. But it's nothing like that. If you don't have a support system or money when you're turned, you won't be able to get any until you start investing. I think that's why baby vampires don't make it. They think the world owes them something, and they get pissed off when they don't get it. Sometimes, we older vampires have to go in and clean out a nest of them when they start changing people because they think they can. That's another rule. They can't change anyone until they're ten years old, and it has to be approved."

"They can't do it, or they're not supposed to do it?" He clarified for her. "What keeps them from changing humans? Is it something in their blood?"

"That's it exactly. Their blood doesn't hold the properties in it to sustain a change yet. They usually end up killing the human by draining them, or worse yet, they're only half-changed and go a bit insane when they awaken. By the time you're ten or so years old, you've come to the realization that being a vampire isn't all that much fun. Especially if you have to be in before the sun rises. That's the way a great many new ones are killed. Thinking that they can step out into the sun like they used to." She asked him if he knew his maker. "Yes, my parents were vampires and had me and a sister. She passed away some time ago because her mate was murdered. They had no children, but they loved each other. My sister couldn't stand to be alive when he was gone from her, so she met the sun."

"That's tragic. I wish I could have met her." He told her that he wished that as well as his parents. "Are they gone as well?"

"My father is. My mother is enjoying her quiet time, she calls it by traveling the world. I think she wanted to do that when we children came along, but the times were just too scary. They could stand the sun, but as children, we couldn't yet. It would be hard to explain leaving your children to rest when you were out and about. That's the reason that they didn't go when we were kids." Calla told him that was so sad. "It is. My father would have loved you. He would have teased you relentlessly with you being a human with a bit of vampire back in your line."

"He must have been really old. I mean, even dying like he did, I'm betting that he's a good deal older than a lot of people I know." Brew told her that was the way it should have been for him to die a very old man and to live a full life. "I want to live a full life with you. Have children someday. I feel I have a lot to learn about being with a vampire yet."

"You do. But we're in no hurry. You won't age, nor will you gain weight, as I told you. And since you have all this time, you can be whatever you want. I've been a doctor and an attorney. I've even worked in funeral homes when I needed some extra cash. Usually, our money was tied up in investments, and when you needed some cash, it wasn't always easy to get to. So taking on an odd job was the thing to do." She asked him if he worked still. "I do. Like you, I think that I'd be bored when I just sat around. With my friends coming to meet you, it will be easy to fall back into the life we had as a kiss, a group of vampires that have no blood relations. I'm looking forward to showing you off."

"I don't want them to feel like they have to treat me with kid gloves, you know. I want

to have fun with them as well." She got up off
the couch and sat near to him. "I only know
what I've read in books about your kind. Is
there a book on—a true book of your kind that
I can read? I would love to have some insight
on it before your friends arrive.

"I have one here." He got up and looked
through the tall shelves of books that were in the
library. As he pulled down a couple of books,
he handed them to her. "You should read all
of these. And if I'm not around, Landon can
answer questions about anything you need as
well. He's been around about as long as Rutger
had, another friend of mine."

Opening one of the books he'd handed
her, she started reading it. Calla knew
immediately that he had written the book. He
started quoting lines from it while she read.
Opening the book for him when he asked, he
stared at her.

"You can read this?" She said that she
could. What was the big deal? "You said you
didn't speak any languages. I forgot this one
was in French. One of the other books is in

Dutch. Can you read it as well?"

They had fun finding books for her to read. She could apparently even read vampire. It was a language that she had never heard of before, and it was quite fun impressing Brew with her abilities.

~*~

Brew enjoyed watching Calla Lily sleep. He would sit with her until she was resting and then stare at her for hours afterwards. The fact that she was his and he was hers made him feel like he'd been in this world just for her. He fully believed that she had been born just for him. And he loved everything about her.

Getting up just as the moon was going behind some clouds, he made his way to her window and stared out. Long ago, he had made friends with the wolf pack nearby, and just tonight, he'd set up a meeting with their alpha. Conri was their alpha leader, which was suitable because his name meant King of the Hounds. Willing himself to the land where he was to meet him, he entered the deepest part of the forest to meet up with the great man.

"You have the scent of a newly found mate on you. It's great that you have someone in your life, old man." He thought that Conri was the same age as he was but had never asked. He had a large family of male wolves, and they were about the best family he'd ever met. "My mate is long gone. It's been too many years since I have even thought of what the flesh of a female of my own feels like."

"That doesn't mean that you're forgoing female flesh altogether, does it? Even if you told me you were, I'd not believe you. Someone must be making your pack very happy, and I know you well enough that you've been out and about in other homes as well." They both laughed, and he asked his friend how his family was. "None of them have mates either, do they?"

"None. My mother believes me to be cursed. She thinks that she'll never hold a child of ours before she is ready to go as well. Father, as you know, was killed some time ago, and we're a better pack because of it." He knew there had been problems with the male elder.

Macky had been trouble for decades before he'd been put to death. "What is it you have a wish for me to help you with? Your mate?"

"Yes. She has an uncle much like your father in thinking that he has no worth unless he's taking her money and slapping her around a bit. The last time he'd put her in the hospital, and that didn't sit well with me." Conri said he didn't think that it would have. "He's currently in jail, but they can only hold him for a few more days before he'll be out again. I don't know that he's killed anyone yet, but I'm having the bodies of his parents reexamined. Calla Lily, my wife, is terrified of him, and with good reason. The bank is on my list as well as they were allowing him to get into her money without his name on the account. There are a few officers as well that I've had a long talk with. I don't believe they'll be doing anything off the books or against the law again. I didn't realize how lax I'd become about the people running my house, either. She fired them all but for Landon."

"If you're planning to hire staff, I have

a few good people who would love to work for a man such as yourself." He said so far, all he had was a cook named Hattie and his man Landon—though he had to confess that he liked Calla Lily more than he did him. "That's the way it should be. He will keep her safe. Is that what you need from my pack? Someone to keep her safe?"

"I can't be at home all the time. And since finding her, it seems like I've only just realized how badly I've been monitoring my funds. She found that I was paying an employee who wasn't working for me at all and another one who has been dead for a decade or more." Conri shook his head, saying that he wished someone would help him with his books. "She's bored with vampire life. Perhaps you can persuade her to keep an eye on them for you. But don't come to me when she busts your chops a bit."

"I shan't. I can have a group traveling your land for you, no problem. But you need to tell your wife. I would hate to hear that she's had to shoot at a couple of them because she didn't understand why they were there. I can almost see this beautiful woman because she would be for you, standing on the front deck holding the fort down while you slumber in your bed."

He laughed and told him that he had no doubt that she'd do it, too. Conri threw back his head and laughed, drawing the attention of most of his pack. Waving them off, he continued teasing him.

"I will send them out this night to keep an eye on things. If you need anything else, just let me know. You've done so much for this pack of mine that I cannot refuse you anything." He said that they were even. "Doubtful either of us feel that we're even. I know that I owe you my life thrice over. And I believe you've been in my healing hut for a while off and on for a while now."

"Yes, we both owe so much to each other that knowing that I'd be able to come to you would make my lovely wife safe so much easier." After a while, the two of them shared a bottle of wine. Brew could drink wine, but it would never satisfy him. Even food sometimes would be something that he'd partake of, but again, without blood, he'd die. Parting ways with his good friend, he made his way home through the darkened woods.

That's when he saw the man lingering through the woods to his right. Not taking his eyes off him, he knew that he'd kill him simply because he was wandering around on his land. The pack land was his as well, but he had been letting the pack stay on it for as long as they wished. It was another thing that he owed the other man for. Saving his ass countless times.

The man moved to the next tree. Just as he was going to leap at the man and tear his throat out, the pack moved as one and leapt on him. There wasn't a sound made, and there was no barking or yipping from the group. As one, they did the job that he really didn't want to do, and it was taken care of. Once the man was dead, there would be nothing left of him, and there wouldn't be a sole to find his body either. The other creatures of their kind and other nonhumans would smell the person, but they'd never tell since it was on his land. Brew was known for being a very fair man and one who could be counted on to hold a grudge, too.

He was just stepping into the kitchen when Hattie showed up in the kitchen. She talked to him for a time about ordering for the household and to tell him that if he needed her, she would willingly give him subsistence to help him. His wife, as well.

"She's a good woman. Loves you too." He told the tiger that he loved her as well. "Good. You've needed someone in your life for some time now, and I'm glad that you've found each other. However, she's afraid. Did you know that?"

"Her uncle?" Hattie nodded. "Yes, I knew. I've made arrangements for the pack to wander through the land to keep an eye on things. Remember that if you were go to out in the night, all right?"

"I'll tell my man too. He said that he saw that the pack took care of a snooper. Some newspaper man trying to get the story on you and your new missus." He told her that he wasn't going to be bothering them again.

"Good to know. I like that about you, Brew. You can be counted on to keep someone safe, and you don't suffer fools well. Yes, I very much like that about you."

Calla Lily joined them, too, and Hattie put a large glass of ice water in front of her. She nearly drank it down; he was happy to see and sat down to tell her about the pack. He didn't want any of them hurt either and was glad that she was happy about having them around. He also said that he wanted her to meet Conri. It turned out that she knew him as well.

Chapter 4

His head was splitting, and he needed something to make himself feel better. It wasn't having Calla Lily around, just the opposite. Having her around made his head and body feel so much better. But it was the constant pulling of the police, Daniel Marshall, and the unknown force that seemed to think this land was free to roam. Three dead now from the pack and it didn't look like an end to it anytime soon.

Brew looked up in time to see that she'd joined him in the office. Telling her what he had going on, never keeping anything from her, he decided that he needed to rest more. When she was sleeping, which she needed as a partial human, he would work himself to nearly falling over until she woke. Then, he would spend the day with her, making plans for their future and neglecting his needs in favor of spending time with her.

"You're looking poorly. I think that even Landon noticed it." He told her what he'd just been thinking. "Good to know. You'll come up to bed with me now, and we'll get this waiting thing over with."

"I don't know that I could be gentle with you. I have had a need for you for some time." She said that she'd had one for him, too, but he's never rested enough to join her. "How long do you think you've been waiting for me to make the first move? I hope not as long as I've been pining away for you."

"Several days, I guess. I've also been worried for you for the same amount of time. Why aren't you resting when you need to." He said that he loved spending time with her. "And how much time do you think you'll get to spend with me if you're dead? You do know that you can die from not resting, don't you?"

"I do. I take it you've been reading the books again. Is there anything about my kind that you don't know?" She said she had four more books to read, but he was distracting her.

"By hanging around with you? I hope that I've not caused you any kind —"

"Shut up and make love to me. Any way you wish." He thought of her beneath him, over him, and sucking his cock. But the way that he thought that he needed to take her was from behind. He needed to be able to control himself and figured that was the only way.

His need for Calla Lily never ceased to amaze him. His mouth crushed against hers, and he took what he wanted. He'd been waiting long enough, his body told him, but his heart said they could and would wait forever.

Her body responded to his need immediately. He lifted her up so that her soft folds met intimately with his hard cock. As soon as Calla Lily wrapped her legs around his hips, he took them to the floor. Pulling away from her, he was on his knees between her legs on either side of him. He rested back on his heels while he looked down at her.

"Take off your blouse, Calla Lily. I need you. I want to fuck you right now." Her fingers moved to the buttons, but his monster wasn't happy with how long she was taking and split the blouse up the back quickly. "I'm sorry. I cannot wait too much longer."

While she pulled her ruined blouse from her jeans, he worked at the snap and zipper of her pants. Standing to pull them off her, he stripped off his own shirt and tossed it behind him. The sight of her in only her bra and panties made his cock jerk hard in his pants.

"Take off your bra. Make your nipples hard for me, baby. Make them ache for me." He felt his fangs drop in anticipation of tasting her. He loved her taste, her scent that she exuded just for him. When his eyes began to turn, her body was outlined in a deep red that made his need sharp. Stripping his pants off along with his boxer briefs, he stood before her naked and stroked his cock while she watched, her nipples beading hard as she rolled and squeezed them for him.

"Brew, please. I need you. I want to feel you inside of me. I want you to drink from me. Make me come hard. Please, baby. I want to feel you come deep inside of me."

Brew knew he wouldn't last if she touched him now. He needed to take the edge off, needed to sip from her so that he would last longer than it would take for him to enter her. Dropping back down, he ran his hands up her thighs and his fingers under her tiny thong. Gripping it in his hands, she looked into her eyes, and he tore it from her body. Her cry of hunger made his fangs burst more through his gums.

"It'll have to be hard, Calla Lily. Fast, hard, and dirty. Roll over for me. I need you too much to do this another way."

When she rolled to her belly and curved her body up over her knees, he growled at her. Her arousal was strong, and he could see her pussy was wet. Pushing her head down to the floor, he nudged his cock at her entrance. She coated him with her juices. Grabbing her hips and pulling her hard back against him, he slammed into her hard and deep.

Her answering groan nearly sent him over the edge. Pulling out to nearly the tip and slamming forward again, he felt her grip around him; her tight sheath wrapped around him tight and sucked him deeper. He felt his climax grip his balls, and the tingle of it run up his spine. Reaching his hand around her front and finding her clit, he pulled hard on it and then squeezed. Over and over, he tormented it until she started to grip him tighter.

"Brew now. Please, I'm coming now. Bite me." Leaning forward, he licked at her shoulder and then sank his fangs deep into her. The hot, spicy blood filled his mouth as she came, milking him and bringing him over the edge with her. As he filled her with his seed, she fed him, nourished him. Sealing the tiny prick marks with his tongue, he pulled her up so that both of them were on their knees, and he was still buried deep inside of her, her back to his chest. Brew pressed his wrist to her mouth and moved slowly inside of her again as she bit into him and drank, bringing her to another climax. As soon as she sealed the wound with her saliva, he tilted her back and took her throat.

Taking enough to sustain him, he licked

her throat and kissed the tiny wound. He held her to his body, feeling her heartbeat return to normal and her breathing slow. He wanted her again, but not now. He would move them to the bed soon.

"Brew, I love you very much. I don't know what I would have done without you all this time. You've made me feel like a new woman." Nodding, he tried to form the words that would tell her what she'd done for him. They were there, but...Christ, he loved this woman.

"And I love you, my Calla Lily. You've given life to these old bones. Given me an outlook on things that I've never felt before." He kissed her on the mouth. "I'm so lucky that you came into my life when you did. I was ready to face the sun, and then you came into my life. I...I love you so very, very much."

She rolled over him when he got them both in the bed. His eyes had never been this heavy, and when he finally let them close, he could feel his body tingling with need. If he didn't fall asleep now he didn't know when he'd get a better opportunity. His body was about as relaxed as it had ever been in his life. His last thoughts were that he hoped his household was safe as he was simply too exhausted to wake up.

~*~

Daniel called the house three times in the last four hours. If he didn't stop, she was going to go down to the station and kill him herself. The man was absolutely batty if he thought that he was endearing himself to her. Calla stepped out on the porch and called to one of the wolves that had been roaming the grounds.

"I need to go and see my uncle." The wolf shook his head. "I know that I can't go alone, but I was wondering if Conri could send someone to go with me. I don't want to face him alone, not that I'm afraid of him, but someone with me could keep me from killing him. Not that he doesn't deserve it, but I don't want to go to prison for his ass right now."

The wolf nodded once and took off. She thought about how far away the pack house was and wondered how long it would take

Conri to come and see her. Or perhaps he'd just send one of his men. She then thought about Brew.

He'd been asleep for the last three days. She wasn't upset or worried about him. Landon had told her that he does this when he's been stressed out and doesn't get the rest that he needs. He told her that he'd been as long as a week in getting caught up on his rest and there was nothing for her to worry about. She wasn't worried, but she did miss him terribly.

"You wish to go and see your uncle, my lady?" Hugging Conri, she told him that she didn't want to, but he was calling all the time. "While there, we'll tell the police to stop allowing him to call you. It will be a simple thing for Brew to do but I'm to understand that he's resting. Are you in need of anything while he is down?"

"No. Landon has told me that he's done this before." Conri said that he had some years ago. "I want him to rest as much as he can. There isn't anything that I can't handle with him down and if it is, I'll simply call to you as

I have done."

"Shall we go?" Conri was dressed nicely. The suit that he had on was beautifully tailored and pen-striped. She loved his tie. When she was close enough to it to see what the pattern was, it tickled her that they were wolves chasing one another in a forest of a tree or two. "I have a car that we can take as well."

Conri didn't clutter her head with small talk. She had been practicing what she wanted to say to him for the last couple of hours. The man was going to be spending more time in jail if he kept bothering her. She turned to the large wolf when he cleared his throat.

"You smell magical. I'm assuming that you've been either practicing it or you've gotten more with the bonding with the old vamp." She asked if it was noticeable to everyone. "No. Just to me, because it is equal to mine and Brew's. You had some before from him, but now you have much more. Have you been practicing it?"

"I don't know what I have, but when I feel it, like bringing things to me, I play around

with it. I can bring anything I want to me —
large or small. I can also make up the beds in
the upper levels. I've been sleeping elsewhere
so that Brew can get a good night's sleep. He's
dead when he sleeps, isn't he?"

"I would say that he'd not like to be
told that. It would bother him that he cannot
be woken if you were in trouble." She said
that she'd not thought of that. "He is a very
prideful man, your vampire. I myself am one
as well. I hope to find my mate someday, but I
don't have much hope for it after all this time.
Brew and I are the same age. But unlike him, I
have younger brothers who are around me all
the time. They're good men, but we're lonely.
Much like Brew was before you came along."

"I love him." He told her that it shows.
"Thank you. I've never been in love before,
and I love the feeling. Having Brew around
makes me feel very safe. These last few days
have taught me that I can take care of myself,
too."

"Good for you." They got into the large,
pale, white limo and headed to the police

station. As soon as they pulled up in front of the place, several officers came out and surrounded the opening door. She didn't know what was going on, but she was glad for the extra security, whether it was for her or for Conri. He told her that it was for him.

"You enjoy the extra as well, but these men are my pack, and they like to make sure that nothing happens to me while I'm visiting them. Not that too much can harm me, but it's a nice perk that I can take advantage of while I'm in town." She thanked him. "No need for that. I do believe that Brew would insist that I have your protection as well. He's a good man in love with his mate, and that's the way that it should be."

She was put into a room with mirrors all around. There was a recording device in one corner and a large table with three chairs. The large ring in the middle of the table, there for handcuffs, she assumed, was another thing that she was grateful for while visiting her uncle. Hopefully, they used it.

The man brought in didn't look very

much like her uncle. The man in front of her, with his wrists and ankles chained up, looked like a man much older than she knew her uncle to be and a mess. It wasn't until he was sitting across from her that she realized that it was indeed him and that he had been beaten up as well.

"Daniel? It looks as if you're getting a bit of what you served me while in here." Conri laughed and didn't bother hiding it from the other man. "What is it you want? And so you know, you're not getting any money, the calls will stop as of today, and there will be no special treatment of you unless they treat you more badly." Again, Conri laughed, and then he told Daniel that he had a few things to say to him as well.

"You've been trying to abuse your so-called power with my pack members. I've given them permission to take you to task when you try that again. Especially the women officers." Daniel told him that they should be down on their knees doing what he wanted. "No one is going to do shit for you, old man. And the sooner you learn that, the better off you're going to be. It stops now, or they'll handle you like they would any other human that bothers them. Understand?"

"What I understand is that you're a dog, and you've been a dog all your life. Whatever you say about them is nothing compared to what I am to you." That didn't make any sense, and both she and Conri told him so. "I know what I said, and I stand behind it. You're nothing but a dog."

"I'm a canine, actually." Conri let a little of his wolf go, and he could see the size of the man. His nails, long and lethal-looking, dug deep into the wooden table and left long scratches there. "You don't want to fuck with what I consider mine, Daniel Patrick Marshall. I will end you with just a swipe of my hand."

Daniel did swallow hard. It was good to see him a little afraid. She discovered just then that she was no longer afraid of him. She wasn't stupid enough to pretend that she wasn't a little leery of him, but she wasn't going to back down right now. Calla was sick of all the shit that he'd been doing to her over the years.

"Now that you've had your say, I'm going to tell you what's really going to happen. You're going to go ahead and pay off my fine and give me some walking around money. Seven grand. It's an odd amount but that's what I've been wanting. Then when the banks are open again, you'll make it so that I can get into your accounts like it was before. I don't want to have to be turned away again, Calla, or so help me, I'm going to cut that ugly face of yours to ribbons." He looked at the officer behind him. "You there. Give her some paper so that she can write this down. I don't want any fuck up from her saying that she forgot something. Give her a nice pen, too. This shit is going to happen, or I'm going to be pissed off, and you know better than to piss me off Calla."

"No." She stood up, and he tried to do the same. "I told you when I arrived, you're not getting any money from me, and I'm not going to bail you out. I like you in here. It means that I can walk around and not have to worry about you coming up behind me for anything."

Conri didn't stand, but she wasn't worried about him. The man was big enough and strong enough to take care of himself. As she was leaving the room, each step away from him making her feel better all the time, she sat down in the bullpen or whatever they called the open station house room and collected her thoughts. It was heady being in charge of herself.

"My lovely bride, how are you?" She nearly burst into tears hearing from Brew. Only she couldn't find him anywhere near her. *"Just think of what you want to say to me, and I'll hear it. I've spoken to Conri and his second, and they told me where you are. Good job on taking someone with you so that I didn't have to kill my good friend."*

"I'm not entirely stupid." He laughed. *"How are you feeling? I hope that you've had enough rest. I don't like being without you for days on end. Also, why would you kill Conri? He's been keeping me company while you were sleeping. I'm so glad that you're awake."* He laughed again.

"I can tell that. Conri is taking care that Daniel understands that as soon as he's out of jail, he'll be

dead. *Telling him that he's better off in there instead of out where I can get him is going to have to make a lasting impression on the man. I have no trouble at all ending his life if he keeps messing around with my heart."* He paused a moment. *"You are my heart, love, and I want you to remember that for the rest of your days."*

Conri joined her a few minutes later, and he told her that he was to take her out to dinner. That Brew would join them. She didn't know how that was going to work but didn't put up a fuss. She was suddenly hungry and thought that she could eat her weight in French fries.

They met Brew at the local hamburger joint. It was a nice place and had been around for some time. Scottie's Den was a good place to get a nice hot meal and to also hear about how the Scotties, the local high school mascot, was doing in the local sports arena. She thought that the local football and basketball were the only things that people around here loved more than they did football on television.

After ordering, her getting a triple order of fries and a burger, she waited while the two men talked. There were things too that she needed to talk to Brew about but none of it was as important as making sure that Daniel knew his place. If she was honest with them, she'd tell them that she wanted him out of her life in a permanent way. Right now, she couldn't care less if he was killed while in jail, so long as he didn't try to hurt her again.

"Calla?" She smiled at Conri. "I must leave now. I've had some things going on at the pack. I would like to extend a visit from my mother. She's been wanting to meet the woman who tamed Brew. She believes you to be saint-like for having to put up with him daily." The three of them laughed.

"I'd love to meet your mom. You told me that your father is gone, correct?" He said that he was indeed gone. "Good. Maybe when this thing is over with Daniel, then I'll come around to see her."

After Conri left them, the two of them talked while she ate. Never would she have thought that she could finish the fries, but she'd not been eating as well while Brew was down, and it was nice to have him there while she enjoyed her food. The malt that she got while there was better than she'd had in a while, and it was made with chocolate ice cream and darker malt. Enjoying food had never been something that she partook in, but this was fun.

"Conri had a talk with Daniel before he left. You know that he's going to be killed when he leaves the jail. Not so much for what he's done to you but for the things that he's been doing to the pack members that are working at the jail. Especially the women." She asked what he'd been doing to them. "Mostly ordering them around and the like. Twice, he's touched them in an improper manner that has their mates upset. They'll have a first swipe at him."

"Wolves are very jealous, I heard." Brew said that they were and that it would get someone killed if the mates weren't together very long. "I hope someday that Conri and his brothers find mates. I bet they would be good mates to their partners."

"I believe you might be right." They

talked about things that were going on around town. With it nearly being summer break for the kids, they were out looking for jobs to do through the summer. The town was sort of down on its luck in some areas. The season for summer fun was heating up, and the pool was being worked on so that it would be ready when the kids started to show up.

The two of them walked back to their home as Conri had taken the limo with him when he'd left them. She did wonder what sort of trouble he had going on at the pack. Brew had mentioned that he would help him if he needed it. What surprised her was that he'd not turned him down but said that he might well need him. Whatever the man wanted from her as well, she'd give it to him. There was no way that she was going to let him have trouble, and she not help him in any way that she could.

Conri was a good man and seemed to be a good leader. He'd been leading his pack for some time now, and from what she'd heard, he was doing a very good job of getting more work for the people and being able to retain his younger pack members, unlike a lot of packs that she'd heard about.

The two of them spent the rest of the evening going over paperwork. He'd put her on all his deeds and investments, and she had done the same for him. There was a great deal of money that he had and hers, while to her was a lot, it wasn't nearly what he had in his accounts all over the world.

"This account is very old, but it has been a good investment. I've been using the proceeds to help around town instead of reinvesting it into the company. I do believe that the way that the company is going, always updating its working schedule, it will be around for a bit longer. Also, we're invested in a lot of smaller grocery stores. There are a few of them around here that we have." She asked the name of them and he told her. "It's good to have a place like these to just pop into them to get something that you might be missing. I don't know if I've ever used them, but they are great to have around."

"I've used them a great deal. But just

because things are on the shelf of the cheaper store, that doesn't mean that they're cheap either. You have to watch every penny to make sure that you're getting a good price." He agreed with her. "Did you know that there are some stores that buy things from the dollar store and put them in their store for double the price? I've seen that happen in gas stations a few times. Little toys for the kids. I can see parents buying them to keep the kids quiet while they're going on the trip. It helps the store's bottom line to have things like that in the store for the kids. They're the worst at buying things that aren't really all that good of a price."

The two of them enjoyed talking about different things. She wasn't as well-read as he was, but she could hold her own in a conversation. They also played chess, another game that she wasn't all that good at but enjoyed. Brew had had decades of practice while she'd only had about five or so years of it.

They ended up on the deck before going

up to bed. She was able to spot a few of the wolves that were about, and she was glad that a couple of them came up on the deck to look around. Brew told her that it was good for them to get her scent so that they could find her if something were to happen to her. She gladly let them lick her hands when they came up a few at a time. She'd not realized that there were so many of them patrolling around.

"I think they sent more over just in case. You can tell the pack members from the wild ones in the pack. I never realized that when Conri said he was the pack leader of the wolves, he was the pack leader of the wild ones as well. I wonder how they communicate?" It was something that they talked about as well, but the conversation got silly after a while, and they were laughing hard by the time they were called into dinner. Calla would still giggle a couple of times at something that was said, but all in all, it was a great evening after having Brew gone from her for so long.

Dinner was a steak and potato. Brew didn't eat the potato, but he did enjoy the steak. His was a little more rare than hers was but that was fine too. She was beginning to like the rarer steak than she had before, and the two of them talked about her magic while she enjoyed a nice pudding. It was one of her favorite desserts. Hot-cooked pudding, still almost too warm to eat. And only in chocolate. Brew called her odd, and she agreed with him. Things that she ate were a bit on the odd side.

After dinner, they retired to the living room. Brew had some paperwork that he had to keep up with, and when he left her in the room, she got another book to read. So far, she'd been able to go through some of his paperback books. Most of them were science fiction and a couple of his romance books. He told her those were for reference, what people were saying about their kind in the books that they wrote.

"No one has it all right, for which I'm glad. There is one person, I do believe him to be a vampire, who writes good murder mysteries. The vampire is a detective who solves crimes committed by supernaturals. He doesn't always get it right, for which I'm glad, but he does get his man in the end. I get his books delivered to me as soon as they're released. And I can read them in just a couple of days. I believe that you'll find them in the office rather than the library. If you'd like to read them, I do believe that Landon reads them as well." She asked him if he'd read them all, too. "I do believe he reads them as soon as I'm finished. It's a nice way for the two of us and now you to have a good conversation about them. I do believe that you'd enjoy them a great deal."

"I'll read them. I love a good murder mystery." When she went up to bed, the books, about thirty of them were stacked in order on her dresser. She couldn't wait to get a start on them.

Chapter 5

Sirous loved riding the train. It was a long way to go to see his good friend, but it let him look at the scenery as he got there, and there was nothing wrong with that. It might well be his last time seeing some of the sights, and he didn't want to miss out on that. As the train came into another station, he decided to get off this time and have a look around. It was supposed to be a good place, and he was hungry for something to read as well. Getting off and keeping his hat tight on his head, Sirous decided to take a tour of the brewery that was on this route.

At the last minute, he decided to go to the courthouse. There was something going on there today, and he decided that it might be a good way to use up a couple of hours. As soon as the courtroom was called to order, he knew he'd made the right choice. There was a trial for a woman with two children who had killed her husband and his lover. Nothing not good about that, he thought with a grin.

He listened to the attorney for the young woman and was happy to find out that she said herself to be innocent. She told the courtroom that she'd befriended a man who said that he'd take care of her, and when her husband had ended up dead, the man had disappeared. He only had to wonder for a moment if the man had been a vampire when the woman, Sally, had said that with her dead husband, there was a lot of ash like the man had set himself a flame.

"You expect us to believe that this man out of nowhere came to your aid and then burnt himself up when your husband was dead." She told the courtroom that she didn't have any other knowledge of what happened to him. He had promised to take care of her. "Yes, we heard about you suddenly having money and a house. Quite convenient if you ask me. And you've no idea that he was going to do that for you, I'm assuming."

It was on the tip of his tongue to tell the

court that the man had been a vampire and that the woman Sally had been his mate. In the little time that he'd met her, not only had he made sure that she had all she needed, but he would bet anything that their names were filed as man and wife in the courthouse as well. That more than likely wouldn't go over very well, not with her current husband being dead, but that was something that was easy for him to look into. At the break, he decided to do just that.

Not only did he find that it had been done, but that the little girl and boy had been registered to the vampire as well. He knew of Salvator Henry but had never made his acquaintance. It would be a shame after all this time for him to lose his mate after waiting so long to find her, but there was little to nothing he could do about that. Sirous would, however, do all he could to help the vampire's mate and children so that they could get all the gifts of his estate given to them.

The first thing he did during the break was to find out where he'd been killed. After finding one of the older newspapers, not only did he find that, but he also found that Ben Trussell had been shot several times in the head. That couldn't be right. If Salvador had killed him, it would have been easier for him to have gutted the man or removed his head rather than to have a gun. Something was off about that.

It didn't take him long with his digging to find the real killer. The man, Ben, had a gambling problem. And his bookie was the one that had killed him when he'd not come through with the money that was owed to him. He would have loved to have been able to dig deeper into the plot, but the train was only going to be in town for another few hours, and he wanted to be on it when it left. Whispering in the ear of the attorney for young Sally, he was able to have the man look into things and get the woman off death row. By the end of the day, not only was Sally reunited with her children, but the paperwork was filed on the house that she'd live in for the rest of her life. He was ever so glad that he'd been a lawyer recently and been able to put the right words into the attorney's mind to get the job finished.

It always surprised him when attorneys were so slacking in their jobs. This man could have done what he'd done, dug a little deeper into the story, and found that Ben was a gambler who was very behind in his payments to his bookie. Or he could have asked the lady who ran his office what had happened that day. It was all there for him to find.

The vampire, sadly, was in the wrong place at the wrong time and had died. But the secretary had known what had transpired in the office, and the bookie would have been arrested in the first place.

As it was, Sally had been separated from her children, and it caused them all unnecessary stress. As he got back on the train, he saw that the woman was going into her new home, which Salvador had provided for her. Poor man, to wait so long to find your mate only to be killed.

The rest of the ride was uneventful. He did do a good bit more sightseeing and had gone into one more courtroom— It was a divorce proceeding and he didn't get involved in that one. Sirous, did people watch. It was something that he'd enjoyed even before going through the change into a vampire. It was another reason that he'd taken the train rather than willing himself to Brew's home. He was able to see humans and shifters at their best and worse while he traveled around. He also got to try a lot of wines, his favorite thing to partake of while he was traveling.

Sirous forgot to call Brew and tell him that he was going to arrive by train. It was all right, he supposed. This way, he could hang out at the station for a few hours and continue with his fun. The thing about humans that he…well, he didn't enjoy it but did observe it was how they seemed to be oblivious to things around them. A beautiful sunset was missed because they were arguing with their mate. A missed painting because their heads were buried into their phone. The pet owner who no more deserves their love than they do that of their human. Beautiful things. Small items.

Tiny smells that make the world a better place. All missed because humans and shifters alike just forget to look.

There were other things that he was doing on this trip. He was going to smell things like the roses and daisies. He wanted to smell the babies of the world as well. The soft fragrance of baby powder would make his day. The smell of an ocean, its saltiness, made him think of summer days with his family when they were traveling to the new world. He was going to make sure that he heard the operas that were all the rage when he'd been younger. The sound of a bird chirping in the morning before a big storm as well.

Anything and everything that he could feel, too. The softness of a woman's cheek. The feel of a shell in his fingers, the sharp edge of a blade newly formed. His own needs in this ending of his life—for yes, that was his plan to get his senses ready for his death by giving them everything in the world that he hadn't given himself time to sense.

He'd been around too long, he'd decided.

Even if he'd met his mate right now, he'd go on with his plans. He knew, Sirous knew that as soon as he met her, he'd have to let her go. His life had been too set, his ways too long ago made. As a man who had been around for thousands of years, he knew that someone who would come into his life wouldn't want to be around him. Sometimes, he hated to be near himself. It was because of the way that he'd become. Jaded. He was jaded from everything in the world and just didn't have the time to be retrained, even if he wanted to.

The plan was to say his goodbyes to those who had meant so much to him. Brewster, for sure, and his new mate, too. Then there was Rance and Rutger. Yosef and Kenneth. He was going to tell them how much they'd meant to him, then drink a glass of wine in their honor before meeting with his death. It wouldn't be an easy one. He'd have to have someone remove his head. The sun, long since not harming him, would do him no good. It was his head that would be removed that would end his existence, and he was glad that he'd long ago talked his good friend Yosef into being the one to do it for him. Perhaps the two of them could end their lives together if he was of a mind to.

The ride was nearly to its end when he finally found the connection to Yosef. It wasn't like they ever lost the connection, but after so long of unuse, it was difficult to connect with it again. As the connection was made, it brought a smile to his face when his longtime friend connected.

"What do you want? I've no use for sentimental calls right now. Have you heard from Brew? The old fool is acting like he's young again. Found his mate and is acting like we all would benefit from finding our own." He huffed, sounding like they'd been speaking for hours rather than just a few seconds. "The old fool. What would I do with a mate at my age, I ask you? She'd run me to the ground or take all my money. Mates aren't like they used to be."

"How would you know what a mate is like, you geezer? You've nary a reference to go by other than what you have dreamed up in your head." He said he could think about anything that he liked. "Good for you. If you were to find your mate, you'd die of sex overload, from what I hear. Brew wouldn't tell me, but I think he's having sex more now than all of us did together when we were newly turned."

"That would be just like him, too, don't you think? He's never had any sense when he was younger." Sirous called him a liar. "I am not. Remember how he used to take chances with everything? When he was hungry, he'd pay the humans for their kindness. Kindness, my big toe. If they knew what he was doing, they'd cut him to ribbons like he was the monster that he was. What makes him think that paying for a bit of nourishment was good for the humans? They'd just spend it on women and drink."

"Good god, man, you're old." He pointed out that he was older. "Yes, I am, but I've never known a man to act as old as you seem to be right now. Have you ever come to the new century, or are you still living in the one that you were born in? What have you been doing with your life, you old man?"

"Nothing." He huffed again. "What did you want? Did you only call to bust my chops about Brew?" He pointed out that he'd been the one that brought up Brew. "Well, it goes without saying that he's going to get his comeuppance when his mate outlives him for whatever reason."

"What is wrong with you? Did someone stub your toe or something? You're crankier now than I remember." He said he was having a bad day. "Don't take it out on me, you bastard. I called because I'm going to end my life, and you promised to do that for me by removing my head."

That shut him up. Not only did he not seem to have anything to say, but he couldn't hear him breathing either. A good sign that he was shocked to his heart. After waiting a few more minutes, Sirous continued.

"I'm to see the others before I go. Brew has told me that he's bringing them all to him to meet his mate, and it will be then that I have my final wishes taken care of. I've had enough of this world and the people in it, and I want to meet and see my parents again in the other world." Yosef asked him if he was serious. "As serious as my name proclaims. I've called to see if you're still the one that will end it all for me. If not, tell me now, as I wish to have my ending lined up so that I don't have to go looking for someone to do it for me."

"I'll do it. If you still wish it. 'Twill be hard on me, as you might know. You're about the only one that I've ever talked to in the last few hundred years. Are you—no, don't answer that. I know you're ready. You've more than likely been planning this for a good long time, too. I'm betting that you have your will made out and all your things given away before the vampire committee gets their hands on things." He told him that things were lined up for him. "You're leaving it all to me? That will set some asses on fire, don't you think?"

"I know that you, of all people, will do as I have asked and make sure that the money goes where I want it to. I had been going to ask

Brew, but with his new mate, I figured that he'd be too busy right now." Yosef huffed. He was better at that noise than anyone that he'd ever met. The man made it his life's work to be the best at it, too. "There are only a few things that I've left undone, and I figure that you would know how to take care of them when the time comes."

"And what if you're like Brew and meet your other half while you're with him." He told him that his plans were set and that he wanted his life to end no matter what. "Well, I'm not going to hold you to that. If you meet her, and I'm not saying that you will, then I'll leave you be. You deserve happiness or whatever comes from having a mate more than most. You've had a rough life, my friend, and I don't want to begrudge you something special."

"Special? It sounds like a great deal of work. He's in New York with her now instead of Ohio, where he belongs. She's dragging him all over the place and spending his money. We both know he has a great deal of it. And he'll spend it all in the first decade. Then where will he be?"

"Now you sound like me." They both laughed. "Nay, I want you to know now that I'll not do it if you find your mate. If she spends all your money, then that's the way that it should be. You broke with a woman that has it all. I'll do it only if you have no mate, and that's where I stand on things. You can't change my mind, so don't even try."

The rest of their conversation was about the trip he was on. Yosef had been a kiss leader in his time, something that he didn't think the rest of them had done. He'd complained about it from the moment the first vampire had moved in and still complained about it today. He thought that his good friend would continue to complain about it well into the next few centuries as well. It was what made him love the old man, his way of turning anything good into a complaint.

~*~

Calla had been warned about the release of her uncle. She wasn't as afraid as she'd been about it, but she wasn't stupid enough to think that he was going to die on the steps of the police station, either. The things that they'd found out about him were vast, and she didn't understand how he'd been free all this time in the first place. He'd murdered several people who hadn't complied with his demands of helping kill her off.

"I should have told him that I can't die but to remove my head." She'd been talking to herself for the last hour while weeding the herb garden. It was nice to be out in the sunshine and doing something productive. Hattie was making her comfort food for dinner tonight, and she was looking forward to it. "That's what he'd do too. Remove my head before I have a chance to see him bleed out." The wolves told her that he'd not get close to her. But she knew better than to think that was going to be that easy. He'd get by them in some way, and that would be all she wrote.

"Have you found all the little tabs to sign?" She'd forgotten about that, to sign off on the last of the paperwork for Brew. After telling him that she was going to do it right now, she looked at how much she'd gotten done and how much more she had to go. "Go ahead and finish it. I know you want to."

She laughed and told him to join her. But he couldn't. He had a meeting with his attorney that he couldn't miss again. He'd been doing that a great deal since she'd come into his life. Missing meetings and phone calls to spend time with her. She'd told him just yesterday that he was going to miss something that she needed to do for herself if he kept that up and decided that he'd stick to his schedule. Calla pointed out to him that they had the rest of their lives together and that missing a few hours here or there wouldn't matter that much in the long run. He begrudgingly agreed with her.

The garden was looking good when she finally went into the house. Hattie and Landon were off tonight, and she was going to have a cold-cut sandwich. Understanding why the others had stopped eating, she was bored with having to have a meal all by herself. She was going to have to get her some friends so that they could join her once in a while for a meal as well. However, she did enjoy giving Brew his meal. Christ, it was like every day he'd find new ways to make love to her that would bring her over the mountain of relief more and more.

"I have two things that I have to get taken care of." She was surprised to find Hattie in the kitchen when she went into the house. "Did you know that I can order food for the house and not have to go to the store? I'm thinking that I'm going to love that. And as you have your friends over, we'll be cooking more. Oh, I baked you some of those cookies that you love. Also, the second thing. There is a farmers market on Saturday mornings in Zanesville. I'm going to be heading up there for some of the herbs that I've seen there before. We'll trade them out of the garden once I get them. And the market, now you're going to love this. They have coffee and tea there that you can serve to your new friends."

"I don't have any friends." She told her that she didn't have any friends yet. "Yes, well, I don't have any yet. You really think that I'll have some soon?"

"You're a wonderful addition to this town. Well, you've been here before but now people are going to want to get closer to you because you're queen of the vampires. You do know that his lordship is the king, don't you?"

"He never mentioned it." She said it would be like him not to tell her. "I thought that he didn't care for a kiss."

"Oh, he doesn't. But that's not the same thing. He's the king of all the others, and a kiss is where a bunch of them will live together in a single dwelling. It doesn't work out too well, them all being so old and sometimes mean, but Brew he doesn't live with anyone but you. And when his friends come to visit, he did tell you about them, didn't he?" She told her that he had. "Good. When they come around, it won't be a kiss but a friendly get-together with them. And they're about as nice as they could be, according to Landon. He's looking forward to it as well."

"Well, good." She didn't know what to think about having visitors, but she wanted Brew to have whatever he wanted. As they talked about the other things that the market had, she was excited to go there and pick up some flowers for the house as well. Calla loved having flowers all over the house, inside and out. "What time do they open?"

After working out the logistics about the marketplace, the two of them decided that they'd go together. It would be a nice way to get up in the sunshine, and they served fresh donuts as well. It was only Thursday, so she was excited about the weekend.

For the rest of the evening, she and Brew sat on the couch and read their books. A new one had come out with his favorite author, so he was engrossed in that. She was reading a book about herbs that she'd found and was happily taking notes when their front doorbell rang. Landon—instead of being off, he was working in the kitchen with Hattie on the new menu program that they'd found. She didn't care. She loved the food that they were making for her.

"I'd like to see my niece." She was behind the door when she heard the voice on the other side of the door. "I've been told that she's supposed to be married to the man that lives here, and I want to talk to her."

"She's not willing to talk to you, sir. Now, if there is nothing else, I shall close the door in your face. It's much nicer than I really want to do."

The door closed, and Landon looked at her with a broad smile. When he made his way toward the kitchen, she laughed. Brew joined her in the hallway just as Hattie was telling him to knock the man into next month. She had a feeling that was going to happen when the doorbell sounded again.

"You have no right to slam the — who the hell do you think you are?" Landon told him that he was the butler of the house. "If she can afford a butler, she can well surely afford to pay me some walking around money. Tell her to get her ugly ass in here —"

"I believe myself to think that all asses are ugly. I've not had the opportunity to see the mistress of the house, not that I would even if given the chance, but I would say that all people have the same form and shape to them. Why would you wish to speak to her ass anyway? There isn't going to be any conversation with it." Daniel asked him what he was talking about. "You asked to speak to her ass. Also, I'm not sure how you expect anything but her ass to come to the door as it is attached to her. You might say that it's a part of her, but I'm not sure one hundred percent about that."

"Just get her in here." Brew was standing next to her and laughing as well. She'd not known that Landon had such a warped sense of humor, but she loved it. When clearing his throat, Brew went to the door himself. "You there. I don't want to talk to you. You've made threats against me, and I'm going to call the police on you. They already know that if anything happens to me, it's because you did it."

"I'm sure that they do. You were warned about coming here." Daniel said that he didn't take warnings. "Too bad for you. You might well want to have a look behind you, Mr. Marshall. It seems that you were warned by the wolf pack as well to save me the trouble of killing you. I believe that they'll make it harder on you than I will. I would just slice open your throat and be done with you, but they'll I do believe that they'll play with you for a while before actually killing you. Good for them."

"What are you talking about? I'm not stupid enough to turn around and see nothing behind me so that you can close the door in my face again. That other guy did it, and I won't allow you to do that to me again." Brew told him to suit himself. She came around the door when Brew asked her to. "There you are. I sure hope that you've made your final wishes known. You're going to be taking care of me the rest of your life."

"If I've made my final wishes, that means that I'm dead. So how would I take care of you for the rest of my life if I'm dead? Not that I have any plans to do anything for you, but you just said something that makes no sense at all. Again." He told her that he knew what he said and he wanted the money they'd agreed on right now. "We didn't agree on anything, you slimy bastard."

One of the wolves, she didn't know them by sight, came up and lifted his leg against Daniel's pant leg. As the liquid sprayed all over him, the other wolves, there were six of them laughed. She thought it was quite funny, too. Just as she was going to engage with him again to piss him off more, he was gone. Nothing was left on the front step but one of his shoes and the hat that he'd had on his head.

Stepping out into the evening, she looked both ways to see where he'd gone. It didn't occur to her that the wolves had taken him. But in the distance, she could hear howling, and she suddenly knew where her uncle was.

The door shut when she stepped into the house, and she looked at Brew. Landon had gone back into the house, and she didn't want to think about what had happened. Walking into Brew's arms, she was held by him while he spoke to her.

"He'll never bother you again." She nodded. "You don't understand, love. He might not be dead as yet, but before the wolves leave the field that they're in, Daniel will be no more and no one will grieve over his passing. I have an attorney going over his estate, and once that is all taken care of and his clothing is found, they'll make sure that you are given what is left of his estate. There is very little of it, but it will be yours."

"I don't want it." Brew nodded as if he understood her. "Can't we just set up what little there is to go to some church or something? Not in his name but just so that I don't have to deal with it or him anymore."

"As you wish." He continued to hold her, and she loved his warm arms around her. "My friends have all gotten back to me, and they're making plans to come here. I've heard from Sirous that Yosef is in a mood and might well be better off not having much to do with him until later. He's always been a bit of a grouchy person, but he's gotten worse since he's been alone. I was told that there was not even a house to his name anymore. Sirous is coming by train, and he will make his way here when he arrives. He said that he has plenty more things to reflect on before he ends his life. He's making no bones about it that he wants to die."

"We'll just have to change his mind when he gets here." Brew told her good luck with that. "You don't know what I can do to make him feel like he needs a new outlook on life. I'll give it to him, and he'll thank me for it."

"I hope that you can. I've lost a great many friends by them being killed. Sirous is closer to Yosef, but he and I have been in contact with each other more than the others. Yosef, as I said, can be a very temperamental man when it suits him." Calla told him that she'd fix him right up. "I know you can try love, but you don't know him the way that I do."

"I'll get him wishing to have met me sooner. You'll see." He kissed her on the nose, and she told him about the market in Zanesville. "Hattie and I are going, and you should, too. You might find that you enjoy it as much as we do."

"I enjoy anything and everything about you, my heart. I shall go so that I can make sure that you have the best of times. I've been to it before, last summer into fall, and I remember it being a good place to see the beautiful flowers in bloom. I believe at one time, we gathered our pumpkins there as well.

Chapter 6

Rance hung up the phone. It wasn't something that he used all the time, but he knew the numbers when they came up on the handset. Thinking about the things that Brew's mate had told him made him believe that things were about perfect for the couple. Then he thought of his own life.

His parents were both deceased. Rance had no brothers, no sisters. The one uncle that he had had gone rogue about a decade ago and had been put down. He'd never had a mate, no good friends nearby, and the worst part was, the few friends that he did have, other than Brew, were thinking about offing themselves so that they'd not have to be bored with life or go rogue.

His uncle Joe, unlike the other men in his life, had lost his mate. She had gone out for a few hours, and just as he was expecting her to return, her death was felt by the family. His own heart had shattered. Losing someone who was close, especially to a vampire, having spent thousands of years together, it would make a man lose all sense of control.

Joe had gone on a killing spree that was talked about for years after. Even now, occasionally, someone would write about the Great Bleeding as if it had happened only a few days ago. He'd killed nearly three dozen humans. Slashing their throats, leaving them to bleed out. He had killed entire families, single adults with family nearby. It was nothing for him to go into a home and pick and choose the ones that he thought had slighted him and kill them while leaving a bedpartner beside them living. It was one of the reasons that Rance had remained a recluse.

Not finding his mate meant that she couldn't be killed. There were other factors involved in his reasoning to stay out of sight, but that was the one that he would tell people about when asked. But Brew had found his.

Calla had called him just now. She'd told

him that he needed to come to the house to celebrate life. Calla had also told him that if he didn't show up that she would come for him, and as she had recently figured out, she was the queen of his kind, and she wouldn't make it easy on him. For some reason, he believed her.

There was something else that he believed about her. While she'd not said anything, she had indicated to him that she would beat his ass if he decided not to do what she'd asked — it wasn't really a question, but if he didn't do what she wanted, he was going to be hurting no matter how she put it.

"We're having a nice wine-tasting party next month." He told her that he only drank reds. "Good for you. We'll have reds and whites, all the colors, and if you only drink the one color, you're going to have a great deal to choose from. However, being here is important to me. Do you understand what I'm saying to you, Rance?" He told her that he did.

"You want me there. However, I don't know what is going to be going on in a month, so I don't know what I'm doing." She told him that, of course, he did. In one month, he was going to be at Brew and her home, tasting wine. "You don't understand. I have—"

"No, it's you that don't understand. Now, as I was saying, we're having a lovely wine-tasting party, and you will need to be dressed up. Black tie. I hope you have a tux. If not, then we can figure one out for you. If you bring a date, he or she will need to be in black tie apparel as well." She laughed. "I almost forgot. If you bring someone who wants more than just wine, we'll have small plates as well. Lots of things that I've been playing around with since we came up with this plan. So you don't have to bring a date that needs to only drink while here."

He tried once again to tell her that he had no plans of going to a wine-tasting party or any other kind, but she cut him off, telling him of the other parties they were going to have, not giving him any dates. Just telling him that once he moved to this part of Ohio, he'd be close enough that he'd not have to stay with them unless he wanted to.

After hanging up over an hour ago, he still was thinking about how he'd been bullied into going to Ohio by a mate to his best friend. And not only that, but by a human as well. When his butler came into his office, he asked him if he was all right.

"I don't know." He told him what had transpired with the phone call. "She's very pushy, I believe, and I'm actually looking forward to meeting her."

Bradford laughed. Rance told him that had she been a salesperson, he might well have purchased all that she was hawking and wanted more from her. They both agreed that they'd never get on her bad side as she might well hurt them, even for being as old and magical as they were.

"I should like to meet her myself, your lordship. She sounds like someone that your father would have enjoyed talking to." He agreed with him and smiled. "So when are you leaving? I'm assuming that you are leaving here soon?"

"I have a month to appear, and then I don't know what will happen." He laughed again. "She threatened to come here and take care that I showed up on time. Bradford, she seems to think that I'm going to be staying with her and Brew in their big house before getting one of my own to live nearby them. Isn't that the strangest thing?"

"It 'tis. So shall I begin closing up the house for you? A month isn't all that long to be able to move yourself and the household there. Or will you be keeping this place as another rental?"

He was telling his man that he should have things closed up within two weeks when he realized what he was doing. Not only did he have a list of things that Bradford could do to expedite his move, but he also had a list of his own to call the bank and other establishments around them that they used. He'd even gone so far as to tell the staff they could have pay for another month after he was gone to help them along. Rance leaned back in his chair.

"She's bamboozled me." Bradford

quietly left the room after not saying a word. As he was sitting there, thinking of what she'd done to him, he wondered at the others who had been in their group. Did she do the same to Kenneth? To…he thought of her bullying Yosef and wished that he'd had the presence of mind to ask about the others who surely would be there for the party.

It took him about two hours to get his mind straight on what she'd done to him. She'd not used compulsion on him. He would have realized that after ending the call. She'd only told him what he was going to be doing and didn't take no for an answer. She didn't even take maybe as an answer either. Wondering at the power of one so young, he laughed until he was crying. His thoughts on what she was doing to his friend Brew was making it difficult for him to walk. Much less breathe.

While making the necessary calls to close up his home, he would catch himself laughing about the young woman. He also wondered again and again if she was just all bluster on the phone or if he could be able to enjoy her wit when he met her. He had a feeling that not only was she keeping Brew on his toes, but she was more than likely keeping him laughing, too. He could almost hear her telling him about the call with him. Brew would be impressed first, and then his humor would kick in. He'd be having a good time hanging out with her like he was looking forward to doing.

By midnight, he had all the paperwork ready to be signed and closed off. He'd had a great deal of his father's things finished up as well. It had taken him a long time to get his father's things gathered up as he'd been living overseas and hadn't thought of getting things prepared at all. He'd not only not left a will, but he'd not made any kind of arrangements for not just the house but the other lands and places that he owned. Thanks to the vampire committee, it was just a matter of him signing his name to all his deeds to have them turned over to him. The money, a great deal of it as it turned out, was his as well after disturbing what he wanted taken care of. His staff and that of his mothers were let go when they decided that they didn't want to be living in the grand house any longer. Then, he sat down to read over his will again.

He'd made one up and sent it off to his attorneys just after his father had died. The only reason that it was still in his possession was because he'd not sent it back to his attorney. He decided it was high time that he did that in the event that he got himself killed on the way to Ohio. He'd never been one to think that he was going to die because he never left his house. But with all the traveling that he was going to be doing, he had to think about those sorts of things.

There were already several changes that he needed to make in it so that when Brew was in charge of his estate should he turn to ash, he'd not throw up his hands in frustration and not do anything that he wanted. As he went over it, marking the changes, he thought about what it would be like to have a mate.

She'd be insane or have to be if she was his mate. He was entirely too set in his ways to bother with women of this century. They were independent. Mouthy and strong. They knew what they wanted and didn't care if you got it for them or not. If they wanted it, they knew just how to get it.

They dressed how they wanted, too. He'd seen more different clothing on women in one day than he remembered seeing when women were walking about town. They used to dress up to go out. Took pride in what they looked like. He wasn't saying that all women didn't do that today, but the few that he did see that were out didn't look like they'd brushed their hair, much less gotten out of bed in time to shower. He didn't like the modern woman of today.

Then there were the kids of today. While he could see the advantages of having a cell phone all the time, he didn't think they understood that there was a whole life of colors, scents, and sounds that they were missing by having their faces buried into their phone.

There were incidents where they walked into trees, cars, and benches. He saw a baby, who was not very old, sitting in a stroller with one of the devices attached to their pram while the woman had one attached to her ears. It was a shame, he thought, that more people didn't just close them off, put them away and enjoy life. That made him laugh.

He knew that he wasn't enjoying life either. But he'd been around long enough that he felt that he'd seen it all, from cars to planes. He'd seen the fastest trains to jets zooming through the sky. There had been times when he sat on an ocean liner, the only way to travel from one country to the next for months on end. He'd seen things too.

The Eiffel Tower. Rance had been there when a president had been murdered. The stage had been playing their roles when someone came in and shot him. He'd heard of boats that carried hundreds of people and had a pool on the deck for them. Things were both strange and new. Things that even to this day, he didn't think could be toppled but usually ended up being so.

Rance thought about traveling to Ohio. To visit or to stay would take him no more than a few seconds with his magic. He could travel by bus, car, or even plane if he wanted. Things today were terrifying and wonderful.

Going up to his bedroom, closing all the curtains and windows, he laid down on his mattress. It wasn't all that comfortable anymore. He couldn't even remember the last time that he'd bought something new. He was going to do that first thing in the morning. Not only was he going to buy himself something better to sleep on, but he was also going to buy him something to wear that wasn't a suit. He'd been wearing black suits with a black tie for longer than he could remember. Christ, he was fucking old, he thought to himself. Too old for a lot of things.

Sleep eluded him. Getting up and walking to the window, he decided to have a seat there. Watching the deer that played in his back yard, he thought of times when that was all he could feed from. The natural wildlife had saved his life on more than one occasion. Realizing that he was getting miserable with his thoughts, he decided that he was going to think happy thoughts for the rest of the month he had until he was to show up in Ohio.

"Like that's going to bloody happen."

~*~

Brew loved the smells that were surrounding him. He could find the scent of vanilla and remembered a time when women would use it as their perfume. Going into the kitchen, he found Hattie baking cookies and his Calla Lily decorating them. She had a fine hand for it, he could see.

"I'm having a burger with fries for dinner. I know you won't eat, but will you please sit with me while I have my dinner?" He said he would go to the ends of the earth for her. "Just to the dinner table is fine. Did I tell you that I've still not been able to get in touch with Yosef? I think that he's avoiding me. That the others have told him that I'm pushy or something."

"You are a bit pushy. Since I've brought you to my home, you've become very good at getting what you want. Did you really make the little boy that delivers our newspaper bring it up to the porch?" She pointed out that he was making an extra twenty bucks a week to do that. "So I heard. He's quite the envy of all the children around town. Also, I heard that you hired a lawn crew for the yard. I didn't think it was large enough for a *crew*."

"I hired two men to help out and their sons. The two families haven't had a job between them in ten years. I thought that if we could spread a little of having money around, more people would take pride in their own yards. You have to admit that some of them are completely overgrown with weeds and cars." He nodded, watching as she put a happy face on one of the cookies. "I also hired some of the pack to help out around the house. Hattie has vouched for them, and it helps out the pack, too. They're not drowning in debt, but it's difficult for them to keep their jobs when everyone in town seems to have a problem with them being shifters. I had no idea that was still an issue."

"We need a new influx of younger people in charge of things going on around the town. If you could do that, have some of the thirty something year olds taking over some of the offices, I believe we'd have a better town, too." She asked him how old the mayor was. "I believe him to be in his late seventies. I remember him when he was but a child and I didn't care for him then either. He's running the town like it's the eighteen hundreds, and he's the sheriff in town."

"I've also noticed that the library is having trouble with getting people to use it. If this keeps up, there won't be enough people to fund the thing come election time." He told her that he thought that it had been on the last election to have more money poured into it. "Did it pass?"

"I don't believe that it did. That's why the building looks as if a good wind would have it crumbling down atop them." She asked him about books. "I don't know the answer to that. I'm assuming that the same books are on the shelves as the day it was opened. You're right in saying that people don't use it much anymore, but I have complete faith in you and that you're going to take care of it."

"There are a lot of things that are on their

way to the dumpster. Or something like that. Did you notice the grocery store has burnt to the ground? Several years ago? The only place that people around here can stock up on things is the Dollar General, and that's not exactly close enough for some people who need to walk there. Don't even get me started on prices either." They talked about how a grocery store had been planning to come to town, but Covid had hit, and all kinds of things that had been in the works had been put off. "Hattie was telling me that jobs are hard to get around here, too, since the basket company went belly up. I know there is one in town, but I don't know enough about it to know if they're hiring or not."

"I don't know either. I tend to stay out of the way of new businesses in town. I know that I should take better care of being informed, but I have been feeling sorry for myself and haven't done much of anything around here. I plan to change that." She thanked him. "You're so very welcome."

He watched as she spread icing on one of the broken cookies and popped it into her mouth. He didn't want to say anything, but watching her eat made his cock hard. It didn't matter what she ate, though when she ate fries, it was all he could do not to jump her. He would feel like she was taking little nibbles of him at the same time. He needed to stop making love to her hourly, she told him, as she was exhausted all the time. Brew just couldn't get enough of her.

"Tonight, we've been invited to the mayor's home for a tea party. His wife is having the tea party, and her husband is having a cigar smoke off. I haven't any idea what that means, but you're supposed to come with me. I don't know what I'm going to do there anyway. I can't stand tea no matter how many flavors someone puts into it." He laughed, enjoying her honesty more than anything else about her. "There will be five couples, not including the Jacksons."

"Who are they?" She glared at him and told him that was the mayor's name. "Oh. I'm sorry. I did mention that I've been out of the loop for some time now."

"You'd have to be about dead not to notice all the election signs all over the yard for the upcoming election. Also, so you know, I've convinced Mr. Candace to run this year. I've banked him a bit so he can afford signs, too." He didn't dare ask who that was, but she seemed to understand that he didn't know him. "He's the vice principal of the high school. He's only in his early thirties and has some good ideas for the town. One of them is getting the library back up in shape."

They talked about all kinds of things that needed to be taken care of in the town. He knew that she'd lived here for some time now, but she seemed to have a better handle on things than he had, and he'd lived here for over two hundred years. Then she pulled out her list. She was forever making lists and handed it to him.

Looking it over, he was shocked to find his name on a couple of buildings. Apparently, someone had asked him if he'd sponsor the building getting the repairs it needed, and they'd put his name on it. There was the Smith

Five and Ten that was still up and running. Also, there was a building that would resell clothing that was donated, and the money would go for baskets in the fall for people who didn't have enough income to support a holiday meal much less toys for their children. Landon remembered it being about ninety years ago that he'd been asked, but for the life of him, he couldn't remember anyone coming to him about it.

"Must have been in your feeling sorry for yourself phase." Brew told her that it was his depressed stage. "You might well have been depressed because you were feeling sorry for yourself. I've seen you pouting around when I'm busy. You need to find yourself something to do that doesn't involve chasing me around the house."

"I was not pouting around the house." She ignored him, and he wanted to beat her butt. However, when he'd tried that on her last night, she seemed to enjoy it more than he had. The things this woman could get him to do was — "What did you just say?"

"I said that you have an appointment with your attorney in the morning. Apparently, it's been set up for a month now before I came along." He didn't remember that either. Another appointment was made when he'd been depressed, not pouting. "He called here to confirm it, and since I don't have access to your calendar, I didn't know what to tell him."

"I don't have a calendar." She glared at him again, but all he could think of was how sexy she looked for him. "I don't know that I've ever had one. I've done just fine on my own."

"Says the man who missed two meetings this week when he was out chasing his wife around the woods." She laughed and told him that she loved him. All he could think about now was how much fun that had been. Calla Lily was up for just about any adventure and fun.

The last three nights, he'd made love to her outside of the house. It had been taking a chance, he knew, for her to be seen by the pack, but that, to him, made it more fun. While watching for a wolf to catch them, he'd not only taken her against the tree but had eaten her pussy until he thought he'd die from the pleasure of it. Christ, she was almost too much for him. And he'd never been so healthy as he was now.

He didn't need to feed daily, and with her being his mate, he didn't have to wander too far for sustenance. Calla Lily was forever up for whatever he had in mind, and she had some great ideas herself. She was everything that he could have hoped for in a mate and more so. Christ, he loved everything about her.

"I do have some things that we need to go over before my friends arrive." She told him that she'd be done with the cookies soon. "There is no need for you to rush or anything. I've decided to buy some of the houses around town and have them fixed up for them. That way, they can move right in once you've bullied, I mean, convinced them to stay."

"I did not bully anyone. I was nice, but I didn't take no for an answer." He said that he'd heard her with Rance. "Yes, well, he needed to be bullied. I believe that he was going to be holed up in that house of his when it fell down around him. His butler, Brandon, said that they've had more water dripping in from the leaks than they do to cook with. They'd have to buy more buckets. I guess his staff still eats. Anyway, he said that the roof needed to be replaced and that the garage that held the cars fell into itself last year, and no one had even called the insurance company."

"You've called them all but Yosef, correct?" She told him that she'd not been able to get in touch with Kenneth either. "He's out of the country on a mission that he's been doing for years. He takes used clothing to other countries and gives it to the people who do not have much in the way of anything, much less clothing. Also, he builds houses in places where they're needed. Of all of us, Kenneth is the kindest person. He works hard and does whatever he can to pay forward anything that he gets from people. You should see his warehouses. He had pallets of things that he could ship out at a moment's notice. For places that have seen destruction and mayhem that has taken lives."

"I might like him best of all. Please tell me that you help him out with his endeavors?" He said that all of them did, sending him anything and everything he needed, including millions of dollars to help out annually. "Yes, I'm going to love meeting him. I bet he might be too busy to come here. That would be sad, don't you think?"

"I think that if you asked him to come here, he would move mountains to come. He's a good man and a better friend than I've ever had." She smiled at him and leaned in for a kiss. "What was that for?"

"For being the best husband in the world. I'm going to have fun setting your friends up with women so they can find their mates. I need women friends, and they're going to help me get them." He asked her if that was all she wanted. "No, I want good friends like Kenneth. I was bullying friends like your friend Yosef. All of them are going to find their mates like we have, and they're going to be so happy that none of them will meet their deaths so long as

I'm around. I need...you and I need them in our lives, and they're going to come to realize that as soon as they find their other halves."

He wasn't sure that her plan was going to work, but he decided that he was going to help her in any way that she asked him to. Even if they didn't find their mates, it would be wonderful just to have them around. Someone that he could hang out with and talk to about the old times. Yes, he would do whatever she needed of him because he loved her.

Brew walked into town to find the houses that were on his list. He decided that he was going to offer them to his friends but not force anything on them. The very fact that they would be close was enough for him to know that the next step in getting them close was having fun again. He'd almost forgotten what fun was like, and he resolved never to forget that again.

The first three houses were a bust. They should have been torn down a long time ago. When he pulled up the listing for them, he could see that even the realtor had become lazy. The picture that was on their website for them had them looking nearly brand new and not the falling down upon itself places they were now. He really had been slacking in this town, and he was going to bring it back to being alive. Right now, it resembled a town on its last legs, and it needed some good blood put back into its bones. Even the school, now that he had time to look it over, looked as if it needed not just a complete overhaul but torn down and started again. It was that bad. But he was determined to make this place somewhere that he could be proud to call home. Yes, he thought, he and his lovely mate were going to do great things for their little town.

Chapter 7

Calla was enjoying herself using the industrial power washer. It was taking the grime off the stone building like it had been a small layer rather than decades of deep dirt. The men who were working on the house had allowed her to play around with it, and she'd not had this much fun in a few weeks. While the house was being washed, the inside of the place was being scrubbed and cleaned.

"Lady Smith?" She looked up at the man who had been in charge of the work in the kitchen. "Hattie asked to have extra outlets put on the walls over the counters. I didn't think you'd mind that, but she wanted to make sure that you approved of it."

"Hattie would know more about what is needed in the kitchen than I would." She did thank the men with the power washer as she made her way into the house by the back door.

"Oh my, I know you told me it would look worse before it would look better, but this is terrible."

"I have to agree with you there. They've been moving my pots around, too." Hattie laughed when she picked up the largest skillet that Calla had ever seen. "I got me this one in the event one of them men working calls me Miss Hattie. It makes me sound like one of those southern girls working in the kitchen. Boy-o, I'm going to enjoy cooking in this here kitchen when it's done. You think that'll be soon?"

"I don't know. It looks like it might take decades to get things back to usable." Hattie laughed again. "Why are you in such a good mood? I would think that you'd be crawling up the walls right now."

"This is all going to make it so that I can have them pretty ladies that you're forever talking about coming into my kitchen and having nice long talks. I'm going to make lemonade and little cakes for them. You're going to have the centerpiece of the house with this kitchen do-over." She asked her what else she was planning. "I'm going to have me some chickens too. I already asked your husband, and he said that whatever I wanted to do to make you happy. Them eggs will be so rich that you'll not believe how good they make a cake taste."

"I hope you're right." She looked around the mess. "There aren't any walls right now. Not to mention flooring. I thought that we were going to have stone floors in here."

"They have to even up the floor in here first. Those other people that you had working here have already ruined the floor where the television was. Walking to the fridge to the set has plum worn a rut in the floor." Hattie had the best laugh. It wasn't a great laugh, but it was loud and made a person know that she surely thought something was funny. "Once they get that all worked out, you'll see them putting the floor that we picked out in place. You don't know how much it means to me to have a say in what goes in this kitchen. It's going to be the best one in the world."

Right now, all she could see was electrical wiring, no counters, no fridge nor was there any kind of pantry. It was being put in right now. She hoped there was a reason for the large opening as right now she and Hattie were the only ones that were enjoying the place. The other two men in the household weren't. She shivered when she thought of all the time and money that was being put into this house at her say-so. Calla wondered if Brew was regretting saying yes that the house needed a major renovation. She only hoped that they'd have money when the house was finished.

The upper levels were being done, too. The whole house was being set to rights. Even the roof was being replaced. Everywhere she looked, there were people pulling out walls or putting them back up. Going outside, she made her way to the little garden that she'd put in a few weeks ago to get away from the noise.

She was sitting in the pretty flower garden, weeding out some of the weeds that had popped up over the last few days, when Brew joined her. There were so many colors in the garden that she was sure that a rainbow had fallen into it and had shared its hues. Glancing at him, she looked back at the garden to finish her task.

"It's too much." He sat down on the bench that had been recently put in. "I know that it's going to look really good, but for now, it's just too much. If not for this place, I might go insane with all the hammering and noise."

"I understand more than you can imagine. It's been so quiet in my mundane life until you came along. I've forgotten what a great deal of noise can be like with what you were talking about. I believe that is why I've been so happy. The little bit of home sounds got me used to them. Now it's all noise, and I don't like it either." Calla told him about the sounds of the electrical equipment. "I agree. The buzzsaw gets me the most. Like it's going through my ears. My hearing is much better than most, so I hear it like a blade going through my head. My goodness, it's terrible."

"I'm glad I have someplace to go like here. Do you?" He told her about his place in town, which he runs off to when things are really bad. "You work there, I guess. I've seen you bringing home files from when you go out."

"I have some things to tell you about. It's about the pack." She asked him if it had anything to do with her uncle. "No, he's gone. No it's about the people that are on the land. I don't know that I've had this sort of trouble before. For the last several nights, there have been as many as six people losing their lives on our land. I don't know what they're doing, and neither does the pack, but they're causing trouble with the land that we rent out to the pack as well. Conri told me that they've lost two of their men out there roaming around." She asked if he was upset. "No, he didn't say he was. Pissed off if I know him well enough. He doesn't like killing anymore than we do, but they've been on his land as well."

"And you don't know what they want." He told her about the letter he'd gotten in the mail the other day. Something about his land being for sale. "Is it? I mean, are you portioning it all off so that you can get more money for the house?"

"No, I could redo every house in the village and still have more than enough for the two of us to live out the rest of our days. I don't want to sell any of it. It would mean neighbors, and I most assuredly do not want that. I'm sure you don't either." She shook her head and looked up at him. "I'm to meet the man in a couple of hours. It's in town, so I thought you'd enjoy going with me to get out of the house. I know that I do for a little while. Also, I was told that the house could be ready in as little as a week. I thought that would cheer you up."

"It does." She stood up and dusted the dirt and weeds off her pants. She'd been told to wear jeans outside in the dirt in case something wanted to bite her. It wouldn't kill her, but it might itch a little before it healed. "I need to get a few things from the greenhouse as well. My flowers need something in the water to make it so that they last longer. Landon said there used to be flowers in the house all the time before they just stopped doing that as well. I'm going to grow as many as I can. Then there is the greenhouse that we put in as well. We're still doing that for the house, correct?"

"Yes. I didn't even miss them until you mentioned it. I loved the scents that it leaves around the house, too." He held her hand as they walked toward the house. She could hear the sounds of work being done and was now thinking about how much Brew was able to hear. She couldn't wait for the house to be finished and was glad that they had the money to do the entire house all at once instead of stretching it out over months. It was difficult to believe that it had only been a few months instead of years.

A couple of weeks later, Hattie met them at the back door. "The first delivery came today. I'm so glad that the kitchen is finished." She asked if it really was finished. "Oh, my yes. I've been unpacking things for the counters, too. Landon has hired a few of the pack to come in and break down the boxes as well. They're just a bunch of teenagers, but they're doing a good job." She showed them around the kitchen.

There were things in the place now that she couldn't wait to use. She only drank water with an occasional glass of wine since meeting Brew, but the hot cocoa machine looked like something she'd use daily. Then there were the things to cook with. Most all of them had been put on the shelves in the pantry to hide them away until needed, and she loved that it opened up the kitchen counters that way as well. The entire back end of the pantry was used for staples such as flour and sugar. The walk-in freezer was going to be handy, too, when they started bringing in the things from the garden. That wouldn't be until next year when they were able to put a garden in, but she was looking forward to it as well.

"I've just heard from Sirous. He's been able to carve out some time to come and visit us in the next couple of days, and then he must go back. But he said that he'd be here for the party." She was excited to meet all his friends, Sirous especially. He was the saddest of them all, and she had it in her head that she wanted to save his life. Sirous needed to find his mate, and she was looking for a single woman to come around to meet him.

She knew that wasn't how it worked but she needed friends like he needed a mate. It was very nice to hang out with Brew and the staff, but she wanted someone to go out to lunch with who could enjoy a meal with her. The staff could, but they wouldn't. They were more class-divided than she thought that most of the people were at the turn of the century.

Calla loved how they walked wherever they went. Sometimes, even in the rain, having a nice, pretty umbrella like the ones in the crock by the door would be something that she carried, even when the weather was nice. It kept the sun off her now tender skin and made a fashion as well. The little one just for her head and shoulders that had pretty little daisies on it was her favorite. Then there was the one that looked like it had cats all over it that were smiling and made her laugh every time she saw it.

Today, she was carrying the little one that had frogs on it. She was picking the newer ones up when she saw them in the stores around town. She swore that they were buying them just so she'd come by and purchase them. Not carrying what they did, she had a nice array of them to choose from when she wanted one to carry around.

"Do you remember me telling you about the money that we have in the local bank?" She said that so her uncle couldn't get to it. "That's right. The banker wants to know if you'd like to combine the two accounts that we have so that it is all in one space. It's entirely up to you, but I told him that I'd ask you what you wanted to do."

"I never thought about it, to be honest." He said that he didn't think that she had. "I guess it would be all right. However, I need to have something that I can spend my own money on in case I want to purchase something for you without you knowing. Something that I might love to get you." Brew told her that they'd leave them separate then. It would be nice to have a surprise once in a while for him as well. "Good. I love to save money up, but I have to tell you, it's nice to be able to indulge once in a while for myself, too. I was just thinking about the umbrellas that I've been getting. I think the stores are finding them for me to buy."

"They are. One of the shop owners told me it was fun to see which one you'd pick for the day. It makes them feel like they're making you happy. I know that it does me to see you twirling one of them around while you seem to be obvious to the rest of the world but for your umbrella." She laughed with him. "I especially like the one that you have that has the flowers all around it and the bright sunshine on the top of the crown. But this one today has gotten you the most attention."

They met at the diner, and she ordered her usual. She didn't really come in here a lot, but they did know Brew, and that was why they remembered that she loved their veggie plate and hummus with cottage cheese and crackers. With a tall glass of water, of course. She was just finishing up the celery when two men and a woman joined them at their table. Calla hoped that Brew knew them because she had no idea who they were.

"Mr. Smith, Mrs. Smith. How are you?" Brew asked them who they were and told them they weren't invited to their lunch. "I talked to you earlier today. I told you that I wanted to meet you about the land that you have for sale."

"I don't have any land for sale." The man laughed, but it was forced. "For that matter, I believe you've been on my land of late as well. You're not welcome, and that could cause you some trouble by trespassing where you're not welcome."

"You have a great deal of land that you rent out to farmers about. I'm going to take the burden off your hands by buying all that land and making it so that I'm the one renting to them. What do you say, do we have a deal?" Brew told him no, just simply no, and told them to go away. When the woman reached for her plate, Calla reacted before thinking about how she shouldn't have. But the woman hadn't been invited to share and stabbed her through the middle of her hand to stop her. When she screamed, Calla pushed her hand away from her platter so that she'd not get blood on it. "What the hell is wrong with you? She was just enjoying the platter for the table."

"This is my lunch, not the platter for the table. A table I'd like to point out that you were not invited to. My husband said that we didn't have any land for sale, and that should be the end of it. I'm not in the mood to make small talk, so take your friends and get out of here." She moved her food to sit in front of her, and the woman used the cloth napkins around the table to staunch the bleeding of her hand. "Oh, do grow up. It's only a little blood. Go to the doctor or something. Just leave is all we care about."

"I've had surveying around the land. What am I supposed to do now that it's cost me all this money?" Brew only leaned back in his chair and sipped his wine. "Not to mention the six men that are still missing and haven't checked in as yet."

"They're dead." She picked up a clean fork and ate some of her cottage cheese. "Also, you might want to know that they've killed a couple of friends of ours and deserved just what they got." Calla looked at the man who was doing all the talking. "You should get the hell out of town while you still can. I have your sent now, and I'm not above hunting you down to kill you as well."

"Did you just threaten me? What the hell have I done to make you say such a thing to me?" She told them what Brew had said. They were trespassing. "That's no reason to threaten anyone. Just tell me to move on."

"I have. Several times, as a matter of fact. You have dead men on your payroll, also you have a lot of equipment that has been destroyed on my land as well. What gave you the right to — will you please take her to the hospital so that she can shut up? I don't care what you tell them. Just get her out of here before I have to stab her mouth closed. Why she insisted to come along is none of my concern." The other man helped her out of the chair and took her out of the building. No more screaming was wonderful. "As I was asking, what gave you the right to come onto my land and think that just because you surveyed it, that I would just sell it is beyond me."

"I was getting the paperwork out of the way. Christ man, how much land do you own?" Officer Peter Lanne sat down beside them with a thick file. It hadn't ever occurred to her that he wasn't human until just that moment. Letting a little of his wolf go, he handed the man a sheet of paper. "What's this?"

"It's a bill for clean up of your men when they were trespassing. The attorney was supposed to be here to take care of this but he thought it would have more meaning if I were to do it. So you owe Mr. Smith here seven grand for the cleanup. Then there is the equipment that had to be taken to the dump when your men left it behind. Of course, I know what you're thinking. They wouldn't have left it behind had they not been killed, but you were on land that didn't belong to you and never would. So here is also a bill for the work that the pack had to do to get rid of the things that were left behind, such as clothing. We wolves don't care to tear up garments, but there you have it. It was a mess to be taken care of."

"I'm not paying this." All Peter did was lean sideways, pull out his gun, and lay it on the table. "What are you going to do, shoot me? For having work done on the land that I plan to own? That's not the way things work for me."

If she'd not been looking right at Brew, she might have missed his changing from man to monster in seconds. He didn't move from his chair, but he did grow his hands and nails out. While it was deadly looking, it cared the man with them—they never got his name—enough to scare the piss out of it. It was a scent that made her think of nastiness rather than anything else that she'd been around. He laid his hand on the other man's shoulder.

"You don't want to fuck with me and mine, Mr. Coulter. That is your name, isn't it? I have told you several times that I don't want to sell my land, nor am I going to. If you're smart, which I don't really believe that you are, you'll leave it alone and go on with your life. However, as I said, you're not very intelligent, and you'll keep pushing me until I have to drain you until you're nothing more than a shell of the man that you are now." Using his considerably long nail, he flicked it across the man's cheek and took the blood flowing to his mouth. "I have your scent now, and I'll have no trouble finding you no matter where you are. Underground, in the air, or just hiding in that house of yours that you think no one knows about. I will find you."

"You're not human." He pointed out that no one in this room was human, not even his lovely wife. "No one told me that when I was asking around town about the land."

"And why would they? They know who takes care of them and why. It's because they keep their mouths shut when it's necessary, and this was, believe it or not, necessary. You'll gather your men and women up and leave town before I have to do it for you. And trust me when I say that my way will end all your lives. Your getting out on your own will make sure that you get out with at least some of your life left. It might not be a good life, but it will be all that I leave for you." Calla ate the last of her carrots and cottage cheese and asked for more water when the waiter came to leave them the bill. "Now, here is going to be what will happen. You get out now, and I'll reconsider what I want to do to you right now. You'll first, of course, pay the bill that I've had written up for you and then be on your way. If I get even a small inclining of you bothering anyone else, I will end your very short life. Even if it's just a thought that you might want to do something untoward, someone, I'll kill you. Or, better yet, allow my wife to do so. She's young and inexperienced, but it might be fun for her to learn being a killer with you."

"You're insane." He said that he wasn't, actually. It was quite brilliant. "You can't just talk about killing me like it would be nothing at all. I'm a human being and I'm not a monster like you are."

"You see, that's where you're wrong. It wouldn't be for me. Anything at all, I mean. I don't care what happens to you. You've come onto my land, did things that caused my wife and me trouble, and then thought that I should bend to your wants when I have no intentions to. You'll either die by our hand, or you'll do as you're told and get out of town while you still can. And by that, I mean, I. Will. Kill. You."

Picking up her fresh water, she sipped it much like Brew did his wine. The man was shaking now, his hand no longer steady like it had been before Brew told him that he was going to kill him. Standing up when Brew did, she watched the man cower in the chair he was in. like he was thinking that he was going to die right now. Instead of acknowledging him, the two of them, Brew and herself, left after paying, leaving a hefty tip after leaving the mess of the blood like she had.

She would admit to only him that she was afraid of the man. Stupid people did stupid things, and she wasn't sure just how stupid the man was. He could be smart, but she doubted that. As she was leaving the place, opening up her froggy umbrella as it had just started to sprinkle, she had a feeling that it wasn't going to be the last time they heard from the man.

Nor would he live all that much longer if he had it in his head that he was above the law and being killed. Peter met them outside.

"He's going to continue. Mayhap not with the land, but I don't think he's going to give up too soon, do you?" Both she and Brew shook their heads. "I'll keep an eye on him if you want but I have a feeling that you have a better handle on him than I can. Just let me know if I have anything to clean up. I think the pack seemed to enjoy having to help you guys out. It was, I know, for Master Conri to help you."

"Your pack leader is a good man, and he will come out ahead soon. I have a few businesses thinking of coming into town to open up some plants. One of them is a large greenhouse establishment that will make it so there are about fifty jobs to be had." He said that would be great. "If you'll tell Conri for me, that would be great. I have a meeting with the company in a few weeks. We'll know then how many actual jobs it'll be."

When Peter left them, he told them that

the bill would be paid soon from the other man, and they walked home. All that they'd come into town for had been taken care of, so they'd not have to worry too much more about that. What they did worry about was the man coming in to cause them trouble, and she worried he'd tell people that he was a vampire.

"I would say that they all know. I mean, they might not know for sure, but they also know that I'm very wealthy and will stop helping them if they try to run me out of town. I'm betting if not now, then soon they'll be having a meeting about that man and making sure that he's out of town before they say a word to Mr. Coulter about what we are. And I don't know if you realize this or not, but you're about as much vampire as I am. The next time we make love, I want to see if you can bite me, too."

"Really?" she felt her pussy gush with need, her body tremble with the excitement. When he inhaled deeply, she looked at his eyes and could see that they turned as well. "I can see your monster. I don't think of him as that, but he is one, isn't he?"

"Only to other people. Never you." He pulled her closer to him and kissed her. She loved this man more than she ever thought possible. When he unlocked the front door, she knew that they were going to go upstairs and make love, but the house was still in disrepair. Christ, she'd be glad when they were gone. All she wanted was some peace and quiet as well as a few minutes alone to think, too.

Brew went to his office, the only room besides the kitchen that was finished, and she went to the living room to find that it was nearly finished as well. The hardwood floors were being installed, and the man doing it told her that it would be done by tomorrow afternoon, as soon as the floor had a few hours to settle. She danced around the hallway, feeling good for the first time in a little while.

Finding herself in the kitchen again, she was glad to see that almost all of the appliances were put away or on the counter. Having herself a cup of hot cocoa to try the machine out, she was sitting at the table when Peter joined her again. He smiled at her, and she smiled back. Whatever was going on, she had a feeling that it wasn't going to be bad but a good thing for a change.

"Mr. Coulter paid his bill. He said that he wasn't going to be coming back here and made it sound like a threat. I don't know, but I think that he was threatened a few times by the locals for spreading the news that you and Brew were vampires. I don't think anyone in town cares so long as they get no trouble from you. And after all this time, I'm assuming that there will be no trouble from either of you." She said so long as they could all live in peace, then they'd get along fine. "Good, that's what I heard too. Also, you should know that the banker in town, I don't know why he told me to tell you, is going to be retiring soon. He thinks that Brew, at the very least, would have a better person in mind than he would to replace him. I told him that I'd tell you guys."

Hattie offered them both cookies that she was just finishing up baking. They were her favorite, white chocolate chip macadamia nut cookies. There were also snickerdoodles, too, that Peter seemed to enjoy. She ate hers with her cocoa, and he had a nice cup of tea with Hattie and Landon. It was an enjoyable afternoon, and she was glad for the company. Even though they'd not go into town and have lunch with her, this was as close as she was going to get what she wanted, she thought.

Chapter 8

Brew knew that the house would be ready tomorrow, but right now, all he could think about was having his mate. Calla Lily was there for the picking, what she called it when he needed to feed, and he didn't want to wait a bit longer. It was now, or he might hurt her when he did take her.

Going out onto the deck that had been covered just this morning, he made his way to his mate, letting as much of his monster go as he thought wasn't dangerous. And he could be to her and didn't want that. He loved her and everything about her.

"I need to tell you something, something important. I've never felt as if you were comfortable with me telling you things about my past, but I must do this. I have a ritual that I want to perform with you. It involves me using a family dagger, an heirloom that has been used for centuries when a male claims his mate. Would you mind if I were to use it tonight? It would bond us in ways that would bring us both more magic. Lots of it, too."

"Will it hurt? I mean, very much. I want to use it because it would make me feel closer to you, but I want to be with you forever." He told her that she would be. "Good, then chop away at me. I don't care so long as it doesn't hurt too much."

Brew reached up to her backside again and felt her tense. Instead of hitting her butt again like he had just this morning when she got out of the shower, he grabbed the waist of her pants and ripped them from her. Her silence was deafening. Brew ran his hand up the curve of her ass and then down again. He could smell her response. It was hot and immediate.

"I'm going to enjoy this, taking you. I have looked forward to this all day, and I want you badly to drink from you, make love to you, with you. I want to make you mine, Calla Lily. Over and over again with just the two of us."

"Don't do this, Brew. There are just too

many people around that can hear us. You know how I love to scream. Oh, Brew…please stop that. I can't think when you…oh, Brew"

Her body shifted on his lap as he entered the long crack of her ass with just the tip of his finger. Her moan went straight to his cock and made him need to reach down and adjust himself before he caused serious damage to himself. But he didn't want to stop. He wanted to get her nearly screaming with need before he stopped playing with her.

"You're getting wet, love. I can smell it. Your heat and need are making your scent strong and irresistible to me." He deepened his finger into her, gathering her cream and moving up to her tight bud. "Hummmm, this is where I want to be. Deep in you here, my cock moving in and out of your tightness. I'd like nothing more than to feed from your throat while I make love to your beautiful ass. And as for people hearing us, that's not going to happen. I have magic enough that they'll not come in here nor hear a single sound from this room."

Brew decided that now would probably be a good time to move to something they could lie down on, something with a lot of room. He stood next to the lounge but continued his torment of her body. As he gathered more of her juices on his fingers, he pressed his little finger against her bundle of nerves and entered her with just one of his fingers. She nearly tossed them both to the floor with her jerk against him.

"Brew, please. I don't...I need you there too. Please. Fuck me. Now, please fuck me hard."

"Make us naked, Calla Lily. I want to feel you against my skin. Take our clothes now, Calla Lily, my love."

He was naked. Just like that, his cock was hard and straining from his groin. His body was hot and hard for hers. His fangs dropped, and hunger surged throughout his body. Slowly moving his palm along her thigh and up the curve of her, Brew savored the feel of her skin, the warm silkiness of her as he brought her back to his chest.

"Brew, please, I hurt with need. Let

me touch you, to feel you." Calla Lily was practically riding up on his shoulder, she had leaned up so high. It was all he could do to keep her there, to hold her for his exploration. Slowly, he moved her down his chest, bringing her breasts to his mouth before he let her go any further from behind. He cupped them both and nearly came when she licked the tips and then bit down on his finger and suckled. Leaning over her, changing her position to where she was facing him, Brew knew that he wasn't going to last much longer.

Hungrily, he fed at them, her nipples first, then her whole breast. They tasted ripe and full, her nipples hard pebbled in his mouth. Brew scraped his fangs over them and wanted to bite her, to taste her there feed from her. When she wrapped her legs around his waist, it freed his hands to cup the heavy flesh and bring them both to his mouth to suckle. Her pussy curved around the tip of his cock, wetting them both with her juices. Her small moans and growls were doing things to him he'd never felt before. His blood stirred and heated his body to the point of near pain for her.

With her legs around him, Brew lowered them to the lounge. He wanted more than anything to turn her to her belly and plunder that sweet ass of hers, but the need to be deep inside of her wet hot pussy was driving him to the brink. Her scent, strong with her own need, was making him as close to the edge as he'd ever been in his life.

"Bite me...Christ, I'm so close to spilling my seed inside of you. Feed from me over my heart, Calla Lily. I'll...I will feed from you when we come. I want to mark you, make you mine, but if we don't hurry, we'll—Calla Lily, baby, don't do that, not yet."

She was suckling at his nipple, her teeth, her fangs he could feel now were just to the point of breaking skin, almost but painfully not yet. Brew could feel his heart pounding as he reached for the dagger. The dagger of his family, the one that would make them one.

Brew was of Royal blood, as was his entire family, and he, too, had used this same blade to bond him to Calla Lily. With this, there was a ceremony where they used a family heirloom, a jeweled dagger and, cut a vein over their hearts, and drank from there. This exchange was more of a ritual than a need, but it was still practiced today, especially by the pure-blooded vampires as he was.

With the dagger in hand, Brew sat up and looked down at her. Calla Lily was his mate, his life, and he wanted her consent, not this forced way of taking her. He would take her anyway, but he wanted her to say she wanted him as well.

"Calla Lily, I need you to want this as well. I want you to tell me that you will willingly take me as your mate, please. I don't want this to color our future together."

She stared at him for a long moment, and then she sat up on her elbows. Her need was still in her eyes and her body, but she was looking less needy and more scared as the seconds ticked by.

"What will happen? I mean, between us when you use it? Where will you use it? Tell me so that I'm not surprised when you do." He explained it as best he could while still feeling like his body felt like it might explode from need. "Then what? You put it away for our son to use on his mate? I'm not full-blooded, so he might not be full-blooded."

"Ah, but I am, and he will be because of the blade that I bring onto your flesh. I will drink from your throat, and you will drink from my breast, just there over my heart when I cut me." She asked him if it would hurt him. "Never. I won't feel it because you'll be drinking from me while I make love to you. And that will be what makes us become one for all time. Nothing will kill us, nor will anything be able to destroy our bond. I will love you forever, my darling, Calla Lily Smith."

"Do it then. Take me and allow me to feed from your heart so that all I have will be yours and you the same for me." Brew took the knife in his fist and sliced it across his chest, just over his heart. He felt the pain of it, and his blood began to flow from the wound, but he didn't try and stop it. He leaned down, dropping the knife on the floor beside the bed, and looked her in the eyes.

"I want you to drink from me because you want to. I want you to be my mate because you need me as much as I need you. Love me as much as I love you. If you don't, if you'd rather leave me now, then do it. I'd rather bleed out than to force you into something that I know we will both would forever regret."

Brew rolled to his back and threw his arm over his eyes. If she left him now, he would die. He wasn't being dramatic. He was being honest. Honest with her as much as he was himself. He couldn't do it, couldn't make her be his mate, not if it would cost them to trust.

When she licked his wound, he nearly came up off the bed, taking her with him. Then she settled over his cock, riding him while she drank greedily of him. When he pulled her hair from her throat, licking the path from her shoulder to her pounding pulse, he bit down hard on her, and her richness filled his every pour.

Then, the magic poured over them both.

~*~

She woke when the sun was pouring through their window. She didn't know the time. It could have been evening or morning, but her entire body ached. The sheets were covered in blood, and her pillow from her side of the bed was all over the floor, with feathers floating all over the room. Sitting on the side of the bed, when she realized that Brew was on the floor, she got up and tiptoed her way to the bathroom to see if she could figure out if she was wounded or not. Her body was too covered in blood.

Taking a long shower when she only wanted a short one, she was reaching for a towel when Brew joined her in the stall. He, too, was covered in blood, but he was different than he'd been before. He seemed taller, his body fuller than it had been. He pointed out to her that she was the same thing, not fat, just bigger than she'd been.

"Your breasts are larger, for sure. Your skin, I've noticed, is silkier and smooth. But I think it's your hair that has changed the most. It's black, shiny black with a single white streak like my mother and sister had in their own hair when they were changed. My mom said it was her badge of honor, marking her as a mate to a strong vampire. And he was, my father, the strongest that there was."

She looked into the mirror and liked the streak. Calla decided that she was going to make sure that it showed up in every time she changed her hairstyle. It would be something that she'd show off. Calla told him what she was going to do from now on.

"I don't think you can cut your hair. I don't know why that's in my head, but my family never could. Maybe it's supposed to be a mark as well, something that people would notice about you and not fuck with you. Will you hand me the shampoo?" They'd been taking so many showers that they were going to have to get stock in shampoo and soap. Laughing when she handed him the last bottle they had, he said that it was kept in the linen cabinet in the hall. She went out there after wrapping the towel around her. "Hang on, Sirous is talking to me."

Since willing their clothing away was

so easy, she willed herself into a nice summer dress with daisies on it. Then, rethinking that, she made her have one on that was covered in tiny little frogs.

She had no idea why she liked the little creatures, but she was going to see if she could find some to put in their gardens with their gnomes. Also she was going to see what kind of help they could be in the garden as real creatures. She went downstairs from their bedroom, not remembering how they got there, while Brew spoke to his friend. Calla was just in time to see that Hattie and Landon were going home for the day.

"I've left you some sandwiches in the ice box for you. There are also cold salads that you can enjoy. There is cold wine in the same place for his majesty and a pitcher of water should you wish some." She heard her calling Brew by his majesty but didn't get a chance to ask her about it. "I also put you some cookies in the cookie bin in the pantry. I have to tell you it's nice having such a well-stocked kitchen for a change. The workers said they'd come back tomorrow to make sure that you didn't have anything else you wanted to change. I believe the house is now finished, and they'll be working on the greenhouse over the next couple of weeks to finish that off as well."

"Mistress, I have hired you a secretary. She has started today with your calendar. There are things that she wishes to talk over with you soon." Calla asked why she needed a secretary. "You are Mistress of the Vampires now and will need to coordinate things so that you and the master vampire can work well together."

"I don't understand." She looked at Brew when he entered the room with them. After telling him what was going on, he said that Sirous had told him the same thing. Also that he'd felt the bonding of the two of them. "I still don't understand. He said that you were the Master Vampire. And that I was the Mistress of them. I thought you said it would just give us magic."

"It did, my lady. All the magic of vampires, and you are the master and Mistress of them all." Landon bowed before her and Brew. "It is a great honor to be able to work with the two of you in your new roles of the king and queen of your kind."

Looking at Brew, she asked him what was going on. He shrugged and told her that he didn't have any idea but might know someone that did. She asked him who it was, and then he stopped her from speaking when he put his finger up in the air. Calla didn't know whether to be upset with him or not, but she did wait.

"It's my mother." She sat and waited for him to tell her more. Things were going very strangely, and she wasn't sure what was going on right now. "She said that we've been chosen to be the Master and Mistress or, in other words, the king and queen of all vampires. All of them would include her as well."

"What does that mean?" He just stared at her, but she could tell that he was listening to his mom, too. "Brew, I don't like this. I don't even know what this will entail for us in the future. Do we have one?"

"Yes. Christ, honey, we're going to live

forever or until we give up the new titles that we have. Then we just revert back to being just Brewster and his lovely mate Calla Lily Smith." She looked at Hattie and Landon. They had stayed when Brew had joined her telling her about the call from Sirous. "Now I'm hearing from Kenneth. He said that he felt our bonding as well and is coming home to visit. He said that he has a book for us to read over. He found it in one of the ancient houses that he's been exploring and then buying up."

When Brew pulled her into his arms, she let him hold her as tightly as he wished. She needed it, she thought, as badly as he did. When she asked him if things were going to be all right, he told her he didn't think they were ever going to get any better. He had her, the master position as well as they'd have all they needed in ways of keeping the other vampires in line with what they told them to do.

"I still don't understand, but if you're all right with it, I am too." He kissed her on the forehead and held her again. Once Landon and Hattie left them, they went to the living room to talk about the things that had happened since he'd brought out the blade. Everything had changed in that moment, and she didn't know what to think about it all.

"Will we get paid?" He laughed at her, asking her if she was greedy. "No, just this is going to take time out of the plans that we had going. Like the garden. I know it's not magical, but it's—Brew, what is that?"

The little creatures, about a dozen of them, came in through the open deck door. It landed on her hand when she put it out to point, and she didn't know what to think about it. The little creature looked as if it had come for war, the way that it was dressed.

"My lady. My name is Warner. I am the faerie that will be at your side from now on should you need help. These others, they are mine to command to keep you able to focus on the tasks at hand. We will be at your beck and call for the rest of your days." Another creature landed on Brew's hand as it sat on his knee. It said basically the same thing to him, but she was a female named Winter. "We have served the kings and queens of all creatures since they were born. You, however, are the strongest of all kinds of shifters and vampires alike. We will serve you for all your lives."

"Do you know if you can answer questions for us?" Warner said that he was there to answer anything they needed, even questions that they might have. "Why us? I mean, the blade has been used by the family for generations, I'm to understand. What made it so that we became the couple who would rule?"

You are the Master and Mistress, as you are the strongest ever born. And there are similar such blades from other families used in the same tradition that you two have used it. But as I said, you two are the strongest ever born for the role in which you have been chosen." She still didn't understand and told him so. "You will come to understand as days and centuries go by. What you need to do now is to learn from the beginning of time since there were Master and Mistress."

He touched his head to the palm of her

hand and asked her if he could do anything right now. He had noticed that the gardens in the back needed to be taken care of, and that was one of the many things he could do to help her.

"I would love to have it up and going right now, but isn't it a little late in the year for us to plant anything more in it?" He said that it would forever grow and produce so long as she wished it. She did notice that Winter was talking to Brew, and she thought this might be more helpful than the little creatures knew. "So anything that I need, such as fruit year-round, will be there for me?"

"Yes, my lady. Your wish is only mine to have finished for you." The room transformed into a plethora of fruits and vegetables. "However, you are as much vampire as his lordship is. He, too, will be able to enjoy the products from the ground and field. It will not only make you blend in better but also allow you to hide in plain sight should anyone come looking for you. And they will, if only to try and prove to themselves that they can try and kill the two of you. Which, as I have said, will never happen. We will also be able to protect you so that you'll be forever safe, too."

"I get that you're saying that we're the strongest couple ever born, but he was born generations and generations before I was. Did you have to wait on me to be born before— what happened to the other Master and his Mistress? Did they die? How long has it been since anyone has governed the vampires?" He told her right to the second how long it had been, and then he told them what had happened to the others. "So they decided to give it up because they were bored. I don't see that happening to me. I see where it will be a long time in working to get things right."

"You are correct, my lady. There have been too many generations of vampires running amok, and now is the time for someone to bring them to task. It will be up to the two of you to decide what their punishment will be. And ours to execute what you have decreed."

"Is there a rule book that we can look over?" Warner told her that all the rules were now in their head and the punishment for each of the crimes. "So it's going to be all or nothing with the rules being broken. I mean, there can't just be a set of rules that we have to follow that applies to everything going on, is there."

"Ah, but they aren't black and white. You will know the rules and the punishment, but you will also be able to change the laws to suit your needs. Yes, they are written as black-and-white rules, but you never know their circumstances until you hear both sides of the story." She told him that she liked that. "Good." He looked at his counterpart and smiled back at her.

"He will have more rules than you will because you will be breeding soon, and your children will need more care from you. A child of a vampire pair will not be born a vampire. And until they're twenty-five human years old, they will act and grow up to learn the ways of the humans, blending in. It is so important for them to blend into anything they might be working with. Then, at the age they were to become fully vampire, they will not just take over more duties for you, but they will have their own faeries so that they might learn from an early age what is required of them as your children."

"Will they also be able to know how to punish vampires that need it?" Warner told her that they'd not be able to charge them with anything but only to report the part that they'd witnessed. There are, as you've heard all your life, two sides to every story and consequence coming to them."

"I love that. Two sides mean that we'll be getting the entire story rather than just one side. Thank you for that." He bowed again, his head touching her palm. "Do you all live forever?"

"Nay, my mistress. There will be times when it will be impossible to save you without the loss of life. We are many. The few that we have here aren't even the tip of a pinpoint that we have ready to lay down their lives for the two of you?" She asked if any of them had family that would miss them. "Forever do we have a family when we are born. But they will be missed and honored by having given up their lives for the two of you. You need not worry about them, my mistress. They are ready to do what is necessary, even to the point of giving up their lives for the two of you and any children that you will have."

It was all too much and still not nearly enough for her. Her mind was so full of questions that she couldn't figure out which one was the one that most needed an answer. As her mind began to settle, the faeries were gone, but for Warner, she closed her eyes and could almost see what she was going to need in the near future. It was just to be calm, and she felt the calmness roll over her. She also needed peace, and it seemed to be right there for her to enjoy.

When she woke up, not even realizing that she was tired or, for that matter, asleep, she looked around the room and realized that she was alone in the large room. Sitting up, she was slightly dizzy but otherwise feeling all right. As she was getting ready to stand up, she noticed the band of tats around her arm. They were words that she could barely make out, they were so small. But she did recognize the date as of yesterday and that she was now the Mistress of Vampires. Whatever did that, the work on her skin, it never hurt her at all.

Finding the lower floor empty, she went to the second floor, calling out to Brew. When she realized that he wasn't in the house, she reached out to him and found him on the back deck of their home, just sleeping as she had been. When she found him, the sun was resting on his face, and he had a smile on his face. Like her, she thought, he'd found peace with the things going on as she had.

"I was just thinking about you." She asked him what he meant. "You're to have a child soon. A male child." She put her hand on her flat belly and asked him why he seemed so sure. "I am sure. Winter told me that you conceived because of the bonding. It is necessary for us to have children and raise them in the way that we are. It will be good for them too to know that we've become what we are because we are good and kind people. Also, my mother is on her way here."

"Will she hate me?" He asked her why she thought that. "I don't know, really. It was the first thing that popped into my head. Perhaps that's a good thing that I'm breeding. I'm to understand what it's called. She won't hate me for making her a grandma."

"She already is a grandma." Brew motioned for her to sit on his lap. When she lay down with her head on his chest, she closed her eyes again. "I'm exhausted as well. I have a feeling that for the next several days, we're going to need to rest up so that we have a better outlook on everything that has happened."

"I want to get up and find out what's changed in the garden and the trees, but I'm like you; I'm just too tired to get up and get going. I hate feeling like this." He said that he did, too, but since there was nothing they could do about it, they should just rest up before the others started coming around. "You mean your friends and mom."

"Yes but they'll be your friends as well. I believe that Kenneth will be here first. As I have said to you, he's done the most with his money and his work. I believe he also wants to settle down and have a family of his own. He will with a mate or not, I think."

"He'll adopt." Brew said it was more than that. He'd just bring children into his home to make sure that they're well cared for. He's a better vampire than I am."

"Doubtful, he doesn't have his demons too. I believe that all of us have some kind of problems that we wish would go away." Brew asked her if she meant her uncle. "I do. He's been a pain in my ass since I was a child. I'm sure there are people in your closet the same way."

"There are. I've just not thought about them in longer than I can remember them. But as you said, we have our life together, and we'll be happy." He kissed her again, and she loved him for it. "What do you say we go out and look at the gardens and see what we can get up to in the yard. With all this help, we can make this a showcase of a place in no time. All right?"

She agreed with him and thought for sure that they'd have more time now than they did before. All she wanted to do was to spend time with her husband and have plenty of children to be just like him.

Before You Go...

HELP AN AUTHOR

write a review

THANK YOU!

Share your voice and help guide other readers to these wonderful books. Even if it's only a line or two, your reviews help readers discover the author's books so they can continue creating stories that you'll love. Log in to your favorite retailer and leave a review. Thank you.

AWARD WINNING, BESTSELLING AUTHOR

Kathi Barton, a winner of the Pinnacle Book Achievement Award and a best-selling author on Amazon and All Romance books, lives in Nashport, Ohio, with her husband, Paul. When not creating new worlds and romance, Kathi and her husband enjoy camping and going to auctions. She can also be seen at county fairs with her husband, an artist and potter.

Her muse, a cross between Jimmy Stewart and Hugh Jackman, brings her stories to life for her readers in a way that has them coming back time and again for more. Her favorite genre is paranormal romance, with a great deal of spice. You can visit Kathi online and drop her an email if you'd like. She loves hearing from her fans. aaronskiss@gmail.com.

Follow Kathi on her blog: http://kathisbartonauthor.blogspot.com/